KARATE DANCER

Karate Dancer

DORIS BUCHANAN SMITH

G.P. PUTNAM'S SONS
New York

Book design by Charlotte Staub
Printed in the United States of America
First impression

Library of Congress Cataloging-in-Publication Data
Smith, Doris Buchanan.   Karate dancer.
Summary: Passionate about karate, fourteen-year-old
Troy tries to convince his disapproving parents about the
true nature of the art and its importance in his life.
    [1. Karate—Fiction.   2. Parent and child—Fiction]
I. Title.   PZ7.S64474Kar 1987   [Fic]   89-5957
ISBN 0-399-21464-X

For my son Matt
humorist, artist, martial artist.

1

Balancing on his left foot, Troy Matthews kick-kick-kicked the macrame tassle of the lampshade with his right foot.

"Troy, will you please stop that before you knock over the lamp?" Mother said, looking up briefly from her reading.

Kick-kick-kick, Troy continued. "I'm practicing light contact," he said. "Pun intended," he added, in case they weren't paying enough attention to get it. In a karate match the object was to make light contact with the opponent while still having enough extension to have made hard contact. Control, control. The name of the game was control.

"Troy, you've been asked to stop," Dad said.

With a sigh Troy folded his arms and leaned onto the back of the sofa, which set off the living room from the entry area. "I'm not going to break the lamp," he said. He didn't mention, nor did they, that three weeks ago he'd broken the dimmer switch on the wall with a mis-judged kick. Neither did they look up from their reading. Dad was at the end of a second sofa, which formed an L with the one Troy was leaning on. Mother was across the room in the yellow swivel rocker she called her nest.

"You coming to the tournament Saturday?" Troy asked.

For a moment neither of them looked up. Then they looked up at one another. Finally Mother looked at him. "Troy, you know we're not," she said quietly. "I wish you could accept that."

Something in Troy's gut rolled over, not accepting. After all this time, almost three years, he still did not accept their disinterest in and dislike of karate. Mother returned to the stack of music books which surrounded her. Dad was studying photographs in Audubon magazines, some of which were his own. They were wimps, these parents of his. They would save the whales and save the environment and feed the world's hungry, but they wouldn't come to his karate tournament. They hated violence and they considered karate violent.

"Did you light a candle for Isaac Funk today?" Troy asked.

They looked up again, this time at him.

"Isaac Kauffman Funk, the publisher, died on this date in 1912," Troy said. "Look that up in your Funk and Wagnall's."

Mom and Dad looked at one another again and grinned. They shook their heads and returned to their reading. Unthinkingly Troy stepped to the hall doorway and kick-kick-kicked toward the top of the door frame. The pantleg of his gi popped with each kick.

"Troy, please," Mother said. "Will you go to your room to do that?"

"I'm warming up," he said. "Keven and Nick will be here any minute. Besides, I have to be ready in case those dragoons jump me." He threw three punches, as if one each at the boys who'd hounded him since he changed from the House of Dragons to Cheney's Karate Studio. He'd dubbed them the dragoons. They still believed in the fakery of the Master of Dragons, who proved his powers of concentration by sticking needles into his flesh. Roger Cheney kept the traditions but didn't teach or perform monkey tricks.

Troy turned into the entryway and began a mock battle, quickly dispatching the first imaginary antagonist and describing it in a sportscaster tone.

"A second attacker has come at Matthews with a sweep kick. Matthews sidekicks and breaks the attacker's kneecap. The dragoon tips forward in pain and Matthews comes across with a ridgehand and that's it for that dragoon." Troy repeatedly reversed positions, being first himself, then the phantom second attacker. As second attacker, Troy collapsed onto the cool tile floor and arose as attacker number three.

"Matthews seems to be tiring but has not lost his sharp edge," Troy said, becoming his own opponent and throwing a backfist into the air. He leapt into the space of the backfist and blocked it. His parents were watching now, amused. The phantom opponent punched and kicked. Troy countered, grabbed the nonexistent clothing of the nonexistent adversary, and spun him about and delivered a smashing front kick to the chest. With a whirl he became the just-kicked adversary.

"The force of the blow hurls the third dragoon backward," said Troy the sportscaster. Troy the dragoon hurled himself backward. "Down the hall," he said as he reeled out of sight of the parental audience. "Dripping blood, he reels through the den, the kitchen, the dining room." He shouted verbal accounts as he, the adversary, propelled himself backward through the rooms. "Across the south Georgia marshland and into the Atlantic Ocean," the announcer said as Troy stumbled backward into the entry end of the living room. He crashed into the back of the sofa, fell over it, and slithered onto the carpet.

"Utter defeat," he said, raising his head feebly. "At your feet."

A car horn sounded and he hopped up as the victorious Troy. Swelling his chest and brushing his hands in victory, he opened the door, said, "See you," to his parents, and he was gone, triumphant, into the night.

Except it was still daylight. But no matter. He climbed into the back seat of the burgundy Mercedes behind Keven and Nick. "Did you have cake and ice cream for Franz Werfel's birthday?" he asked. "Franz Werfel, Austrian author, born in Prague on this date in 1890."

"What did he write?" Nick asked as he drove away from the curb.

Keven groaned. "Don't give him fuel, Dad."

Troy's Chases' Calendar didn't list the titles of the author's books, and before he could think of something Keven spoke again.

"Dad has a new gi," Keven said.

"Aren't you going to listen to me list Werfel's books?"

"No," Keven said. "See Dad's new gi?"

"How could I not?" Troy said, crossing an arm in front of his eyes. The gi was red, trimmed in black, and would look magnificent with the black belt Nick would be earning soon. "Hey, Nick," Troy said, reaching over the seat back to clap Keven's father on the shoulder. "Nick, you have a new gi."

"I'm getting ready," Nick said. "Sprucing up."

"I have one too," Keven said. "But I'm not wearing mine until the test. It might be bad luck."

Nick hunched a shoulder and raised a hand from the steering wheel as if to say: What can you do with someone who is superstitious? Troy clucked at Keven's wariness, even though he felt somewhat the same way. He rather favored his own fading black gi that showed he'd

10

been at it awhile. And an unfaded black belt would look sharp on it too. Black belt. Troy grinned to himself. He was going to be a black belt. In just a few weeks the three of them would be going up for their tests. He'd been waiting for this since he first heard the words "karate" and "black belt" on television when he was six years old.

They entered Cheney's Karate Studio quietly and took their places sitting cross-legged, belts in hands, hands in lap. On Mondays and Thursdays they sat thus, in rows according to rank, with the white belts first, then yellow, blue, green, brown, and black. Troy, Keven, and Nick sat with three others on the brown-belt row. Behind them were three black belts.

On the dot of 7:30 Roger Cheney entered from the adjacent office and stood before them. Darius had not yet come. Cheney bowed. The students rose and bowed in response. The knowledge of the bowing had bothered Mother. She said she wouldn't bow to anyone except, perhaps, the Queen of England out of courtesy for the custom. But this bowing was courtesy too, not worship. Students bowed in honor of those of higher rank who had gone before and out of regard for the effort of those who were coming along behind.

In unison, each drew his belt through the left hand by pulling it with the right. Then the belt was wrapped around the gi and tied in the traditional square knot. Next they knelt for meditation, sitting back on their heels. Still Darius had not come. The tournament was Saturday and Darius, who had never been to a tournament, said he was going. He also said he was working on a forms routine, though none of them had seen it. A musical form. Troy cringed at the thought. The musical forms were too much like dancing. He couldn't bear for Darius, his years-long friend, to be so candyass. And the

11

form, music or not, was bound to be a disaster. Darius wasn't even interested enough to come to class on time. Sometimes Troy was sorry he'd persuaded Darius to start class last year.

Troy shook his head to shake Darius out of his mind. He'd felt himself heating up. The meditation was to give them time to consider what they were learning here, a honing of the mind which preceded the honing of the body. The most important thing in karate was learning to think. Control, control.

After meditation they began the warm-up exercises to get the blood flowing. They did jumping jacks, running in place, touching their toes, easy stuff to work out the kinks. Then they began the more difficult stretching exercises. Sitting with legs spread at right angles, Troy gripped his left ankle with both hands and lowered his chin to his left knee several times. As he gripped his right ankle and touched his chin to that knee, he looked under his arm to see if Darius had come. Cheney always started promptly. He refused, he said, to waste the time of those who came on time. He also refused to let anyone exercise or spar without meditation. If you came late, you sat in a chair by the door until break.

They went through the entire stretch-out routine, ending with snapping sidekicks which popped the gi pants like rifle fire. Troy remembered how hard he'd practiced to gain the skill and speed to make that sound. Now he could stand and kick with a repeated pow-pow-pow.

"Okay, you guys. That's enough," Cheney said, and he began the instruction and correction. "Troy, I notice that when you're doing the spinning backkick you need to cock your leg earlier in the spin. It's making your kick late. Your opponent will notice the lag and jam your kick." Assuming the stance, the instructor zipped around

12

and cracked the kick out, fast, straight, and hard. He reset, spun again, and stopped halfway around, knee cocked high, posed to kick. "See? Like this," he said, gesturing to his kicking leg. "Now you try it."

Troy practiced it, spinning, kicking, spinning, kicking. One by one Cheney made corrections for each of them as they practiced leaps, kicks, dodges, feints, fakes, punches. The key to good practice, Troy had learned, was to first be sure you were doing the technique correctly, then repeat the action until it wore groves in the brain, bone, and muscle. The object was to be able to perform effectively without conscious effort. If someone came at you with a backfist, you sidekicked. In a match or in a real fight, the mind should be free to concentrate on the opponent's movements and weaknesses. That meant free from anger, too. There was no room for anger in karate.

While fine-tuning his spinning backkick, Troy saw Darius come in and sit down. On his next kick Troy's pantleg nearly exploded. Pow! Why couldn't Darius get here on time? Pow! In Cheney's classes you progressed or you were out, that was all there was to it. No hassling, no fussing, no giving in to excuses or persuasion. Pow-pow-pow! The House of Dragons substituted ridiculous rituals for excellence in performance. Troy had paid his paper-route money to them for nine months before he knew the difference and changed to Cheney's. Now he called the Dragons "dragoons." Darius might as well be a dragoon. And he knew better. Darius was in Mom's high-school honor chorus, and she demanded their best. Roger Cheney also expected the best. Cheney's students showed well in the tournaments in both fighting and forms. And Darius, Troy was afraid, was close to the "no-progress" limit. If he didn't shape up, Darius was going to be out.

When Cheney called for break nearly everyone lined up at the water fountain. With Keven before him, Troy headed for Darius.

"Hey, man, where've you been?" said Keven.

"Yeah, hey, man," said Troy, mocking Keven.

"Been talking to Molly," Darius said with a grin.

Troy kiaied and popped a reverse punch into the air. "Jupiter's eagle!" he said.

"Yeah, hey, man," Keven said. "I think I'm going to barf."

A month ago there was no Molly and now it was Molly-Molly-Molly. Molly on the phone. Molly at school. Darius couldn't even say her name without grinning. Probably couldn't think about her without grinning, Troy thought. This Darius, whom Troy had known since first grade, was becoming a stranger. And Keven, whom he'd known less than two years, was now the more familiar. He and Keven had forged a bond over karate. Keven took it seriously, practiced every day and, like Troy, was going for his black belt. Troy and Keven practiced together almost every night. Then, of course, there was Nick. Troy's own father wouldn't pay for Troy's classes and here was Nick not only paying for Keven's classes but also going to class himself, alongside his son.

Troy would faint with pleasure to have his father come to class with him. Or do some of the other things Nick and Keven did together—fish, hunt, camp, go to ball games.

Cheney signaled for the end of break by clapping his hands. Everyone resumed position on the floor for the brief second-half meditation. Then Cheney designated Troy and Darius as sparring partners. Troy smiled with pleasure. The first section of the sparring was between unequals, with a higher-ranked student teaching one of lesser rank, helping the one of lower rank to practice.

"Don't forget your PMA," Cheney said. Somehow, Troy thought, his own feints and jabs would infuse Darius with PMA. Positive Mental Attitude. Through force of will he would transfer his keenness for karate to Darius.

Troy arced a ridgehand at Darius and would have decked him but for stopping short. He halted his hand just shy of Darius' jaw.

"Get your block up," Troy said. "Lift your forearm and block me."

"Yeah, yeah," Darius said.

Then like a repeating film frame they punch-blocked, punch-blocked, punch-blocked to drill the block motion into Darius' brain and sinew. Slowly at first, then faster and faster, Troy delivered techniques to give Darius practice. Troy continually moved a degree slower than Darius, being the tortoise, trying to prod Darius into becoming the hare. They practiced punches, kicks, and blocks. Every few moves Troy threw something at his own speed and skill just to keep Darius humble.

"See how fast I can get inside you?" Troy asked. The side of his hand was touching Darius' throat.

"Yeah, yeah," said Darius.

"You have to learn to anticipate and be there with a block. Why are you here if you don't even care?"

"We care in different ways," Darius said.

For the second part of sparring Cheney surprised Troy by pairing him with Nick. This session was between equals in skill and, as much as possible, size. Nick outweighed Troy by far. When Troy first came to the class, he'd had to start over at white belt. Keven and Nick had been blue. But Troy had been progressing quickly and the three of them had made brown belt about the same time. Still, it made Troy nervous to spar with Nick. Nick always three-pointed him so handily that it was embarrassing.

Did this pairing mean Cheney thought he was improving? On the street, of course, an attacker probably would be someone larger and stronger, or someone who thought he was stronger. It was the way of the world, Troy guessed, for the larger and stronger to pick on the smaller and weaker. He tried to settle his turbulence and dig into his reserves of Positive Mental Attitude. He wanted to learn everything there was about karate, mentally and physically. And he was learning, learning, learning.

Nick, he thought, to bolster himself, I'm the best. You're just a candyass. Too soft and sweet!

They went at it then, Troy and Nick. Kick, block, punch, block, kick, block, punch, with Nick's red gi flashing.

"Point!" Troy cried in surprise when an inverted reverse punch got inside Nick's block. But he'd felt his mental and physical control.

"Your point," Nick acknowledged. They stepped back and dropped their arms. "Ready?" Nick asked.

"Ready," Troy confirmed. Quickly, they tangled again. Punch, block, spin, kick, block, punch, kick, block, block.

"Point," Troy said again, amazed and a little flustered at his success. Another reverse punch. He'd made points on Nick before, but never two in a row. "Are you letting me get inside?" he asked as he assumed the neutral position again.

"No indeed," Nick said. "You're just getting better."

They began again, Troy heady with the compliment, with the power of knowing. He really was getting better.

16

He could feel the improvement in muscle, blood, and bone. Soon he would have his black belt, and what a feeling that would be, to have his black belt at age fourteen. The rush of ego made him careless and the next point was Nick's, but the next was Troy's and he had won a match with Nick!

His spirits soared in spite of his effort to contain them. A martial artist did not gloat in victory. Not outwardly, anyway. And Nick might very well win the next match. But he wondered how it felt to be Nick and outmatched by a fourteen-year-old. He wondered how his father would feel if his father knew his son could physically outmatch him? When that realization had come to him recently it had sliced him through with pain. The father was supposed to be stronger. For a while yet, at least. And it hurt to think his father really was a candyass. In spite of Troy's thoughts in preparation for this match, Nick was not.

On the way home they rehashed the match, reviewing every punch, kick, and block, analyzing techniques.

"I just couldn't seem to get away from your reverse punch," Nick said.

"My father doesn't even know what a reverse punch is," Troy said.

2

"I won a match with Nick," Troy said as he burst into the living room. He gave one quick glance out the window and saw the taillights of the Mercedes dotting the night.

"Did you," Mother said, making it a statement, not a question. His parents were sitting as they had been, Mother with her music books and Dad with the stack of Audubons, as if they hadn't moved all evening.

"He can no longer escape my reverse punch," Troy said, jab-jab-jabbing into space. He reproduced the point-making techniques from the match in time with a Bach Brandenburg which was stirring through the room. Dad was paying half-attention, his eyes seeming to move independently, like a chameleon's, one eye on Troy and one still on the magazine. Mother was not looking up at all.

"Read, read, read," he said. "Don't you ever just want to watch TV or play checkers or something?" They looked up then, smiling. "I mean, I'd think that when a person's only son, only child in the wide, wild, wily world walks into the room that the person might even look up and say hello, how was your evening. I didn't bloody anyone's nose or break anyone's arm tonight. It's perfectly safe to welcome me home."

Dad blew him a kiss. Mother set her books aside and

came over to him. "Welcome home," she said, enfolding him in her arms. "I haven't hugged my child today." He kept his arms straight at his side. This "hugging-my-child" bit was something she'd started recently. It made him feel like a bumper sticker.

"Well, I have to get the drawings done for the *Historian*," he said when she released him. "But if you're not going to the karate tournament Saturday, I certainly hope you'll plan to go to Swartz, Louisiana for the Stink Creek Horseshoe Tournament."

"Sure thing. I'm already packed," Dad said as Troy disappeared down the hall.

Troy shut the door to his room and kicked aside some soiled clothing and drew the stool up to the drawing board. As long as he kept the door shut, his room was his own and they didn't hassle him over the shambles. He lifted a fresh sheet of paper from the stack and smoothed it onto the drawing table. He caressed the paper as though the motions would smooth out the knot of bitterness toward his parents' lack of interest in his karate.

They were okay, he told himself. They let him have his room and didn't demand he keep it neat and clean and make the bed every morning as did Darius' parents. Nor did they come in to clean and straighten and examine his belongings as did Keven's mother. And they liked his wit and imagination and were enthusiastic about his art, pleased and proud about his job drawing things for the newspaper.

About him was the room he and Dad had designed and built. Built-in closets, desk, dresser, and drawing table were along one wall, topped, like a broad shelf, by two end-to-end beds. Plenty of space, were it not for the clutter, for karate practice.

His hand gravitated to a black drawing pen and almost

before he knew it he was drawing. Mr. Hutton, owner-editor of the Hanover *Historian,* wanted a cartoon to accompany an editorial about migratory merchants. Here and there around town someone or other would park a truck and commence selling mattresses, meat, tools, trivia. Such vehicular vendors, Mr. Hutton said, were sometimes selling stolen goods.

The pen worked over the paper as lithely as Troy's hands and feet had recently worked Nick over. Before he'd made many strokes he was melded with the ink and pouring himself out onto the page. The brown belt, still around his waist, had vanished from his consciousness. From the point of the pen emerged a slinky, mustachioed villain with a pushcart full of purloined wares.

Troy couldn't remember a time when he hadn't loved to draw. The passion for pen and ink preceded that for karate. He had first held a crayon, his parents said, at age fifteen months and had never scribbled.

Bent over the paper in concentration, he completed the drawing from top to bottom as he went. Some art teachers had tried to teach him to sketch differently, but his new high-school teacher was fascinated with the way he worked and encouraged him to keep it up.

"Each artist works in a special way," she said. "And cartoonists, especially, must work quickly." With her protruding teeth, beak nose, wire-rim glasses, and thick graying hair pulled severely into an enormous bun, she was one of the jokes of the school. Even her name was a joke. Miss Clutz. But she was anything but a klutz. Her hands worked nimbly with whatever she touched—clay, wire, chalk, paint, fabric. And her feet were nimble as she walked, always briskly, through the classroom or through the halls. The open-backed wedgie shoes she wore marked her progress with a clack-clack-clack.

20

When she stopped to survey a student's work, however, there was no hurry in her. She stopped. She looked. She absorbed. She made accurate and helpful comments. Even the unartistic students, taking art for credit instead of love, Troy noted, were amazed at what they could do in Miss Clutz's class.

"We are all artists," said Miss Clutz, whose voice sounded as though she was an actress, too. "All of us are creative. We must be. It takes an immense amount of creativity just to live."

And he, Troy Matthews, had the good fortune to be in her homeroom as well as in one of her classes. In these first three weeks of school, she had asked him to help with several special projects. He admired her second only to Nick.

Holding the drawing at arm's length, he clucked with satisfaction. This was a thoroughgoing improper villain, a real transgressing trader. Troy was sure Mr. Hutton would be pleased.

After setting a fresh sheet of paper on the drawing board, he picked up a sheaf of photos of the Hanover Courthouse on Grand Square. Mr. Hutton wanted a small stylized version to incorporate into the masthead. "The Hanover *Historian,* Reporting History As It Happens." Honed and Hoperated and Hustled by Harvey Hutton, Howner and Heditor, Troy thought, laughing at himself. As he picked up a pencil, he wondered how much Mr. Hutton would pay him for it. Ten bucks for the villain. Twenty, perhaps, for the right aspect of the courthouse. He smiled at the idea of earning money for doing something he enjoyed doing.

His first job at the paper had been delivering papers, before he was twelve. He had not really liked delivering the once-a-week paper, but his parents wouldn't pay for the karate lessons he'd been wanting for years. If he wanted lessons enough to earn his own money, however, they had said they wouldn't say no. They even drove him back and forth until he changed to Cheney's and started riding with Nick and Keven. He'd delivered papers for more than two years when, six months ago, he'd summoned nerve, courage, gall to show Mr. Hutton a cartoon. The editor had jumped at the chance to have original artwork for the paper.

"And at a price I can afford," Mr. Hutton had said. "Surely a thirteen-year-old won't price me out of the market."

"Almost fourteen," Troy had said.

"Well, Mr. Almost Fourteen, how does five dollars per cartoon sound?" Troy almost leapt with excitement. Real money for doing what he did all the time anyway? "At least one a week as long as we are both satisfied?"

"Yes, sir," he'd said loudly, and he'd taken Mr. Hutton's outstretched hand. He'd been tromping Old Town until dark every Wednesday for $7.50 a week, which had just barely covered the monthly twenty-five-dollar fee for his karate classes two nights a week. Mr. Hutton had raised him to ten dollars per drawing and sometimes wanted more than one a week, and Troy quit the deliveries.

In some future year, he dreamed, he would have his own adjacent studios. Above twin doorways would be a broad sign reading "The Arts," and beneath it, above the corresponding doorways, smaller letters would say "Martial and Fine."

3

"**R**ide?" Mom said in the morning.

"Nah," Troy said. "I have to drop these by the *Historian*." He waved the drawings at her.

"I can swing by there easy enough," she said, lifting the papers in his hand to take a look. "Ahh, sweetheart, these are terrific." She grinned and reached up and rubbed his hair.

He ducked from her hand. "Thanks," he said, "but I'll walk."

"I notice you don't ride with me now that we're in the same school," she said. "It's still the same parking lot."

"I like to walk," he said, and he set out. School was not far, four blocks down Duke Street and four east along Queen. Going by the newspaper office added five blocks, but the east-west blocks were quite short. Drawings in a folder atop his stack of books, he headed even farther out of his way, west, toward the river. All the schools were on the same campus and it was true, he acknowledged to himself, that he used to ride with her pretty often in the mornings. But now that he was in high school, her school, it seemed different.

At the river, fog lay thick over the water, marking the path of the channel. Wisps of fog hung in the trees like Spanish moss. On such days Troy was certain he would see the Georgia equivalent of the Loch Ness monster rise from the silver mist.

23

As he walked through the scrubby growth along the river, beggar lice and sandspurs hitchhiked on his pant-legs. South of him was the harbor, where freighters from Taiwan, Rumania, and Sweden plied the channel, whistles wailing for the bridge to open and let them in or out. Also south were seafood-processing plants, mostly for shrimp and crab. Cars glutted the parking lots and hundreds of people were at work inside, but there was no one to be seen. Alongside him, clinging to the edge of the river, were shrimp-boat docks, empty of the trawlers which had left before dawn for the day's work.

Fog pressed flat against the water and fish jumped, seemingly without a splash. The cry of gulls seemed muffled. Troy wondered if mist actually diminished sound or whether it only seemed so. In the fog, this familiar river, the Altamaha, had an air of mystery about it.

Mistery mystery, Troy thought. With just a molecule of imagination he saw the curving undulations of a sea monster beneath the surface of the water. Any moment now the Loch Ness monster would appear. No, he thought, not the Loch Ness, but the Altamaha's own sea creature. There she was now, breaking the crystal face of the river, skimming snakelike along the top of the water. The apparition was forty or so feet long, he estimated, and perhaps eighteen inches in diameter. The front of the serpent rose above the water. She had two protuberances, each set with a huge, fiddler-crablike pop-eye. As Troy watched her, she watched Troy.

And what were those tendrils wavering like antennae from below the head? There were three sets of them flowing out from what would be the neck, except the creature was all neck. As Troy continued defining this creation in his mind's eye the reptile seemed to speak and

24

say her name. "Altamaha-ha," Troy said aloud. "Altamaha-ha," he repeated, calling out the name, leaping with delight and slapping his thigh. His books pitched forward, he lunged, caught the folder midair as the books landed askew. Grateful he'd at least caught the folder containing the drawings, he stooped to gather the books and the Altamaha-ha disappeared into the mist.

And Princess Avenue appeared from it. He blinked in surprise to see he was here, in this real world, in Hanover, and not in some mythical kingdom where sea monsters roved the rivers. There was the usual bustle of activity at Hanover Hardware on the corner of Princess and River Street, but otherwise the town was a ghost town. Banks, lawyers' offices, shops, the library—none of these was open yet. Except for the hardware store, which opened at seven, the hours of the street were from nine to six.

Away from the river, the air was clear. Troy walked down Princess Avenue as though he were the last living person in Hanover. He turned back to look at the river, to be sure that the river mist, as well as the Altamaha-ha, was not just in his imagination. The mist was there, banding the river like a gray velvet ribbon. Facing forward again, he saw a movement ahead, some ethereal motion as though the mist hovered over the street after all, and the Altamaha-ha, perhaps, was cavorting on Princess Avenue. A block down the sidewalk, apparently observing herself in one of the storefront windows, a girl was dancing.

Troy stopped and watched. Two graceful arms swept arcs from above the head to the toes. The girl wore jeans but they didn't restrict her movement. As though suddenly self-conscious, she looked up and down the sidewalk. Just before her eye fell on him, Troy pressed himself against the building. He felt like an intruder, a spy. In a moment she resumed her private ballet. If Troy had ever seen anything so lovely he did not recall it. In the few minutes since he'd left home, the patches of fog had lifted. Except for along the river, mist was evaporating and the day was warm and bright with south Georgia sun. His eyes created mist now, shrouding this girl who was more a mirage than the sea creature.

The courthouse clock bonged him out of his reverie. Before the second strike, he knew it would sound eight times. He couldn't stand here on the sidewalk daydreaming. He'd promised Miss Clutz he'd be at school early to draw some posters. Loudly whistling the flute part of a Mozart concerto, he stepped down the sidewalk. The girl heard the whistling and immediately stood still, as though she was merely standing, waiting, staring into the storefront window.

As he approached he saw she'd been dancing to the newspaper-office window. She was someone he knew from school. Liesl somebody. He plucked at his memory for her name. They'd been in school together forever. He even had a class with her this year, he thought, but classes were still new and he couldn't remember for certain. Yeah. Liesl Trunzo. That was her name.

"Hi. Good morning," he said as he passed her on the sidewalk. He stepped to the doorway of the newspaper office and reached for the knob, which didn't turn.

"Nobody's here yet," Liesl said.

Troy gave her a quizzical look. "Mr. H. is always here by eight," he said.

"Not today he's not," she said. The courthouse clock had just completed the eighth sonorous bong.

"Well, uh, I guess I'll, uh, wait," he said. Why did his insides feel like worms? There was a wide slot in the door and he could slide the folder through. He ignored the slot. "I, uh, have some drawings for the paper," he explained, standing first on one foot and then the other, disobeying his will to be still.

"I know," she said. He flushed. "I mean, I know you draw for the paper. I've seen your cartoons."

"Well, yeah, uh." He couldn't quit staring at the way her dark hair fell forward of one shoulder and behind the other. He transferred his gaze to her reflection in the window but there she was looking at his reflection and their eyes met, shining in glass. He forced his eyes onto the mail slot, then to his shoes. The sight of his shoes embarrassed him. They were so grungy. Just broken in good, he'd told his mother when she tried to buy him shoes for the new school year. Now he wished he had new shoes, or three-week-old shoes, at least. In the midst of the self-consciousness he shifted his glance to her feet, her recently dancing feet. He laughed with surprise, relief, and pleasure. She had on dirty white sneakers with holes worn above the little toes.

"What's funny?" she asked.

"Nothing," he said. "You. Me. Us, standing alone on the street." He looked again at her well-worn shoes, which made her so real, so connected with planet Earth. "You know, I saw you as I came down the street." Her eyebrows arched. "I thought you were a mirage."

"Here he comes now," she said. Troy swallowed at the sound of her voice, which was as fluid and graceful as her body. He looked up at tall Mr. Hutton striding down the sidewalk.

"Well, Liesl, Troy, good morning," the man said, and inserted a key in the door.

"I left my ballet shoes," Liesl said, brushing past Mr. Hutton as he stopped to pick up some things that had been dropped through the slot.

"Well, Troy, let's see what you have for me." Mr. Hutton took the folder from Troy and walked into his office. Troy followed. "These are wonderful. Wonderful, Troy. Perfect," he said of the villainous vendor. He held the courthouse drawing at arm's length. "Yes, yes. You are a marvel. How about twenty-five dollars for the courthouse, half now and half when I mull it a bit to see if there need to be any changes. Liesl, I'd give you kids a ride but I'm riding shank's mare today."

Troy turned. Liesl was passing the door. Ballet shoes more frazzled than her sneakers were tucked beneath her arm.

"That's okay, sir, thank you," she said. "I like to walk and there's still plenty of time."

"What's shank's mare?" Troy asked.

Mr. Hutton patted his feet. "These little ponies at the end of my shanks." Troy heard the front door open and close. Mr. Hutton nodded toward the sound. "She's my neighbor. Helping me with layout. She really has a good eye for it. I hope she has a quick head for headlines. I'd like to teach her that too. It would be a help."

"I have a quick head for headlines," Troy said, immediately embarrassed by the timing of his remark. "I mean, no, I'm not trying to take her job or anything."

"I know, I know," Mr. Hutton said, rummaging through his desk drawers for something. "Say, Troy, can I pay you later? I seem to have misplaced the checkbook."

"Sure, Mr. H., sure. No problem." Troy didn't wonder at the lost checkbook. The newspaper office resembled nothing so much as his bedroom. But here, as there, lost things usually came to the surface from under something or other. "I'll come by later in the week to see what's up for next week."

Already, his spirit was outside, following Liesl down Princess Avenue. He wanted his body there too. On the sidewalk, he saw she was already at the corner passing the Ritz, the old movie theater, which had not been open in his memory. He walked quickly to catch up. By the time he was in front of the Ritz, she was on the circle sidewalk of Grand Square. As she passed the courthouse steps, however, he was almost up with her, so close he could have reached out and caught her dark swaying hair. In three steps he could be walking with her. But what if she didn't want him walking with her?

He walked quietly behind, watching the swing of her free arm, watching the way her hips rotated beneath the faded denim. Everything about her pressed against his eyeballs and stirred his sensibilities. He thought of Darius and Molly and how he'd hooted and teased. Now he wasn't even sure his legs could maintain him upright here on the sidewalk. He could go limp and become a puddle right here on this sidewalk and Liesl Trunzo would keep on walking and never know it. He almost cried out in pain and he stomped his foot to restrain himself.

At the sound of the thud on the sidewalk, Liesl turned, surprised to see him so close behind her.

"Oh," she said. "It's you."

He dissolved and became the puddle, floundering in his self-made lagoon. Right here on Princess Avenue he had become the Altamaha-ha, with emphasis on the "ha-ha." She looked away and continued walking. He realized that he, too, in spite of himself, was still on his feet and moving along behind her.

As she crossed Duke to Queen he wished he had the courthouse drawing back. He would put some people in the picture, himself and Liesl walking along the sidewalk. In front of the Queen Street Bookshop she stopped and pondered the offerings in the window. Now he had no choice but to stop or pass her. His facile tongue was blocked. His facile brain could not think of a single thing to say about books.

"Did you know it was O. Henry's birthday?" he asked, his calendar tricks coming to his rescue.

"What?" she asked, looking up at him.

"O. Henry's birthday. You know, O. Henry, William Sydney Porter, the short-story writer who wrote 'Ransom of Red Chief'? Born this date in 1862."

She looked at him unbelieving, as though she had suddenly discovered he was an idiot. Indeed, he agreed with the opinion in her eyes and hastened to walk away. He heard her steps on the sidewalk behind him, lithe Liesl steps. Lithe, laughing, lethal Liesl steps. He burned with self-consciousness, wondering what she was observing about him. His hair? The swing of his free arm? The way his hips shifted inside his jeans?

"O. Henry's birthday, huh?" she said from behind him. Her words entered his bloodstream and seared him totally in one nanosecond.

"The Stink Creek Horseshoe tournament's Saturday," he said, wishing he could chain his tongue to his tonsils. He twisted his book-holding arm and glanced at his watch. Eight-ten. Had this earthquake taken place in just ten minutes? If he ran he could get one poster done before the bell rang. If he ran, he wouldn't have her burning, teasing eyes behind him. Feebly, stupidly, he turned to her as though they had been walking together. "I have to run," he said, and he ran.

The running, at least, gave him something to do, an excuse to retreat by going ahead. The running was also an excuse for the red face he wore when he pounded up the campus stairway of Hanover Academy. He took the outside stairs two at a time and started up the inside steps the same way. Not quite formed as a conscious thought was the idea that if he reached the art room in time he could look out the window and watch Liesl come up the school steps.

Suddenly, in rapid succession, three arms sliced the air in front of him, each accompanied by a verbal "Kiai." He stood on tiptoe, as though seeing over these arms would get him to the window.

"And where are you this morning?" said Bert, the owner of the nearest arm.

Heat flared inside him and he clenched and unclenched his hand. The dragoons blocked his way on the stairs and he wouldn't reach the art room in time to look out and see Liesl.

"In the middle of a Bruce Lee movie, no doubt," said the owner of the second arm, Dwight, the tall one.

Control, control, Troy thought, wanting to splatter them all down the stairs.

"Naw, don't you know?" said Stuart, who was attached to the third arm. "He *is* Bruce Lee. He just goes around incognito as Troy Matthews so people won't know he is still alive." The three of them stood, arms extended, hands in chop position. When other students approached they folded the arms to let those students pass, then snapped them open again to keep Troy's passage blocked.

"Electronic gates," Troy said, trying for humor instead of anger. "Is that what you are imitating this morning?"

"Don't be smart," the dragoon named Bert said.

"We practiced by candlelight last night," said Dwight, as if the mystique of candlelight somehow increased their skill.

For such as candlelight, Troy had left the House of Dragons for Cheney's Studio. He pursed his lips and

31

shook his head. These three thought they were the Three Musketeers but they were really the Three Stooges. They didn't have the sense to know that with their arms already fully extended they would have no momentum with which to deliver a blow of any force. Even with them above him on the stairway he could kick the knee of the first, leap up with a backknuckle to the chest of the second, and make a spinning kick to the ribs of the third and have them all below him before they knew what hit.

"But can you throw a punch in incandescent?" Troy asked, turning suddenly and trotting down the stairway, leaving them there with their arms foolishly extended. Dumb dragoons.

"Look at the candyass go," one of them said.

"Next time bring your candle," Troy called over his shoulder, and when he looked back he was about to carom into a couple of fellow students. In instant stop, he drew up on his toes and his book-free arm flung out and arched gracefully upward, like the wing-stretch of a shorebird.

"Whoops," he said.

"Whoops," she said.

It was Liesl! He had almost run into her. And there, on his toes with the one arm up and out, his core went hollow and his heels thudded to the floor. She was with one of the older students, Donnie Duggan, who was in assorted important positions around the school.

"Oh, hello," Troy said as his body fell back into a normal posture.

"O. Henry," Liesl said, and they all walked on.

Oh, hello, Troy said to himself, mocking himself as he mounted the opposite stairs. Why hadn't he said her name, to let Donnie Duggan know he knew her. Oh, hello, Liesl, he should have said. Or: Hello *again*, Liesl.

32

"Oh, there you are," Miss Clutz said as he entered his homeroom. "Will you have time for the poster?"

"Sure," he said, sliding the stack of posterboard from her desk and picking up the box full of marking pens. As though there was still a chance of seeing Liesl on the sidewalk, he aimed for the table nearest the window and looked out. His eye fell across the leaves and limbs of live oaks and down onto an un-Liesled Queen Street. He took up the black marking pen and, on automatic, began to draw.

Classmates wandered over and gathered around him, watching.

"What's that?" asked one.

"The Altamaha-ha," he said, just now realizing what it was he was drawing. How would that tie in with what Miss Clutz wanted for Club Day? he wondered. Sometimes his hand scurried ahead of his thought processes. He slid this drawing off the top of the stack and put it on the bottom.

There was a chorus of disappointed "Awws."

"Finish it. Aren't you going to finish it?"

In response to the outcry, he returned the banished sea serpent to the top of the stack. His thoughts caught up with his hand and he began lettering. "The Altamaha-ha says: Join your favorite clubs by September 30." Another inspiration hit and he discarded that sheet and let it slide to the floor as if he were at home.

"You're not throwing it away, are you?" a girl asked. "Can I have it?"

Troy was already off and sketching another Altamaha-ha.

"No," said someone else, picking the fallen poster from the floor. "We're using it."

This time Troy drew glasses on the Altamaha-ha's

33

bulgy eyes and the creature was holding a book in one tendril, to represent the Book Club. With a second tendril the Ha-ha was eating refreshments and with another she was playing chess, moving a rook.

"How do you do it?" someone asked.

"I wish I could draw like that," said another.

The laudatory words drifted over his shoulder as he completed this poster and began another. He was too busy to take heed of their wonder at something he did so easily. By the time the bell rang he'd finished three posters and, since this was his homeroom, he kept drawing. As he finished each one it was removed from beneath his hands by those in charge of posting the posters. Then notebooks, notebook paper, and occasional arms were thrust at him.

"Draw me one."

"Me too."

"Me too."

When the bell rang for first period, students left the art room variously adorned with Altamaha-has. Liesl, Donnie Duggan, and dragoons were all gone from Troy's mind.

4

*T*roy stood at the living-room window watching for Keven and Nick. Dad was leaning over the long coffee table sorting through some night photos he'd taken recently in the marsh.

"Look at these," he said.

Troy had made up his mind not to pay any attention to photography until Dad paid attention to karate. Still, he didn't quite have the nerve to ignore his father. He stepped away from the window and looked. Dad had snapped a raccoon fishing at the edge of one of the tidal runlets. The photos were terrific and before he could remind himself to be quiet, Troy said, "Hey, neat. Are these for an assignment or did you do them for yourself?"

"They're on spec," Dad said.

The pleasure of knowing sprang up in Troy as he returned to the window. He knew what "on spec" meant, not just from Dad telling him but from his own experience. He sometimes did things on speculation for Mr. Hutton, ideas for drawings or cartoons he drew without having the commitment first. If Mr. Hutton's enthusiasm matched his own, the drawings were bought and published. If Mr. Hutton said, "No, I don't think this works," there was an addition to the pile on Troy's bedroom floor.

Troy looked at Dad again. This sharing, this connection produced such good feelings and he wanted more. He wanted this kind of sharing from Dad about karate. He parted his lips and ran his tongue along them, aching to ask one more time. Please come to the tournament. Please take me to the tournament. He pressed his lips together. It would be stupid to dash himself against the refusal one more time.

The burgundy Mercedes appeared at the curb and Troy picked up his gym bag. "I'm gone, Dad," he called. Louder, he called good-bye to his mother, who was in the music room practicing. She didn't hear him. "Don't forget the Stink Creek Horseshoe Tournament," he said to Dad.

"I was waiting for you to remind me what day it was," Dad said.

In the car he announced, "It's Morton Pumpkin Festival Day in Morton, Illinois. It's also Independence Day in Costa Rica, El Salvador, Guatemala, Honduras, Mexico, and Nicaragua."

"Whoopdedoo," Keven said, circling a finger in the air.

"And notice he named them in alphabetical order," Darius said.

"They must have been listed that way," Keven said. "You know he couldn't have put them in alphabetical order."

"You're the one," Troy said. He settled back beside Darius for the hour-and-a-half drive to Jacksonville. "So, Darius, you really came. You sure you can leave Molly this long?"

"She's out of town for the weekend," Darius said.

Troy, Keven, and Nick gave a round of teasing understanding.

"So having nothing better to do," Troy said, "you thought you'd try out a karate tournament."

"Just you wait," Darius said. "Your day is coming. And I promise you one thing. I will never tease you about it."

Troy gave no sign that it had already happened, however short-lived. The vision of Liesl still danced in his head. The eleventh-grade Donnie Duggan superimposed itself over Liesl, however. He'd seen them together several times during the week. And in spite of what he'd manufactured in his head, she was not in any of his classes.

The car rose onto the mile-long Altamaha River Bridge, known locally as the River Bridge. In this Georgia coastal flatland, the bridges were the only hills, this being the highest and affording the finest view. Gulls played in the thermals above the bridge. The silver steel network of the lift span was webbed against the sky.

"Hey, look," Troy said, leaning toward the window. "There's the Altamaha-ha."

"The what?" the others asked in chorus. Keven and Darius leaned to look. Nick kept his eye on the road but cocked his ear for the answer.

"The sea serpent. Haven't you seen it?" Troy asked.

"Oh, that thing you've been drawing at school," Keven said, settling back in his seat.

"Taken again," Darius said. "Troy, forty-four. Sucker friends, zero."

"Oh, come on. Where's your imagination?" Troy said.

"I think it's there in the car next to us," Darius said.

Troy looked and nearly leapt over Darius. "It's the candlelighters! Going to the tournament, I'll bet. I hope they're going to the tournament. I hope I draw every one of them."

"How could you do that?" Keven asked. "They'll each be eliminated in the first match, so the most you could probably draw is one, for the first match."

"I'll take Dwight," Troy said. "The tall one. Go faster, Nick. Don't let them leave you behind."

Nick pressed the accelerator and repassed.

"Roll down the window, Darius," Troy said, but Darius wasn't quick enough. Troy leaned across Darius and deafened his fellow passengers when he yelled, "Did you bring your candles?" Whether the young men in the adjacent car heard the words or not, they looked over. When they saw who it was in the burgundy Mercedes, three of them lifted simultaneous middle fingers.

As they went by the turnoff to Golden Isle, the highway returned to two lanes and Nick remained out in front. Troy turned and gave menacing looks out the back window. Just before the interstate, the car following stopped at a gas station.

"You'll need all the gas you can get," Troy said to them, who could not hear.

"Who are they?" Nick asked.

"Assorted stooges from the House of Dragons," Troy said.

"I told you about them, Dad," Keven said. "They're the ones who keep riding Troy. He was in class with them before he came to Cheney's and they keep trying to show how good they are."

Nick looked around at Troy. "I hope you draw all three of them too," he said. "I hope you cork 'em. What belt are they?"

"Pink belt, I think," Troy said. "They practice in candlelight."

"Yeah," Keven said. "Real candyass."

"Will you please let this candyass off at the next stop?" Darius said. Troy grimaced. Darius did not practice in candlelight but Darius was entering the competition with a musical form.

"If you're ever in a dead-end alley and your only out is

the other side of some badass, you're gonna wish you'd practiced some of this stuff you think is stupid," Troy said.

"I try to stay out of dead-end alleys," Darius said.

Troy slouched in the seat, knees pressing the seat in front, head resting against the soft upholstery behind. He had no more words for people like Darius or his father, who would let anyone run over them. Darius, at least, was here. But it was Nick, there in the front seat with Keven, who kindled his fantasies. Nick, who did active things with his son. Including karate. He felt himself sliding into the silence of self-pity.

"Hey, you guys. Did I tell you that today is the day of the Stink Creek Horseshoe Tournament?" He forced his words.

"Where does he get this stuff?" Keven asked as they groaned and broke into chatter.

Once they reached the gym, Troy's head cleared. At the door their names were checked off and they received their competitor identification. As usual, Keven's name was spelled "Kevin" and he reached for a pen to correct it.

"Oh, we've misspelled your name? I'm sorry," said the gatekeeper.

"It happens all the time, I'm used to it," Keven said. "It's Keven, like seven." Troy and Darius laughed. They'd heard Keven explain it so many times.

Nick smiled and shrugged. "Blame your ancestors. Somebody back there didn't know how to spell." The Keven-like-seven had come down through the family.

Inside the gym, people of all sizes, but not all shapes, were standing, talking, stretching out. Martial artists were usually slender. Strength without bulk was the creed.

Troy's eyes roved the gym. The floor was crisscrossed

with blue tape marking off three rows of four rings each. Taped numbers identified each ring. Troy saw Cheney, who was helping with the tournament. He also saw and spoke to people he'd met at previous tournaments, and pointed out some of the well-known ones to Darius.

"See there? That's Matt Smith. He's been written up in the karate magazines. One of the best middleweights around." Troy breathed deeply. The air was clean and fresh but soon it would be thick with body heat and the smell of sweat. This odor of physical exertion was an elixir to Troy. Such was his natural habitat. Leave it to the raccoons, he thought, to prefer the bank of a marsh creek.

"Hey, man, looka there." Keven pulled Troy by the elbow.

Troy followed Keven's eyes and there were the dragoons, coming into the gym in full regalia. Dwight and Bert and What's-his-name. The fiery Dragons all had yellow gis. And two of them were wearing brown belts.

"I can hardly wait," Troy said, slamming the heel of a hand into the air. "I'm going to bust ass."

"What's this?" Cheney said as he joined them. "Whose ass are you after?"

Troy jerked his head toward the mock-musketeers. "Those guys," he said. "They're with House of Dragons, where I first started karate. Ever since I changed over to your studio they've been trying to show me how much better they are."

"Are they?" Cheney asked.

"No, sir!" Troy said.

Someone called Cheney and he held up a hand to indicate "just a minute." "Then you don't have anything to prove, do you?" Cheney gave Troy an encouraging pat on the arm before he walked away.

40

"No, you don't," Nick said, also patting Troy's arm. "But you're going to prove it anyway, right?"

"Right," Troy said. It was so good to have Nick's backing and support, especially compared to what Dad would say. Dad would say, "Walk away." Walk away indeed! "Those guys have been agitating and agitating until you'd think they were washing machines. I'm going to knock them right into the spin cycle."

"Hey, man, yeah," Keven said. "It will be easy enough to draw one of them in the first match."

"There will be a bloodletting," Troy said.

"And you the bloodletter," Darius said.

"Oh, come on, Dar, it's just talk," Troy said. Anyone who drew blood in the tournament was instantly disqualified.

"What you practice is what you do," Darius said, quoting Cheney.

Troy laughed. He was surprised to know Darius had even paid enough attention to quote Cheney. "Well, I haven't actually let any blood lately," he said. "I'm behind on my quota."

"Where's the dressing room?" Darius asked. The form competition was first and he had to change into his gi.

Troy turned a thumb toward the dressing room and resumed watching the dragoons. If they were entering the fight competition it would be easy to get a match with one of them. Though they used the term "draw," there was no actual draw. Competitors stood around the ring and the judge walked along the line and paired you with the person standing next to you, unless you were from the same karate school. Competitors from the same school often wound up in a match, but never in the first rounds.

An announcement from the loudspeaker asked for all

but the forms competitors to please clear the floor. Troy, Keven, and Nick climbed into the stands to watch. Troy settled himself on a bench with his gym bag between his feet. The forms, called katas, were similar to the floor exercises in gymnastics. A competitor could use a traditional kata or do an original one and, like the fight competition, they were done by belts and divisions. Forms competitors were graded from the moment they stepped into the ring, and were judged on balance, grace, power, speed, coordination, agility, and accuracy.

There was no way to keep track of everything at once. A karate tournament was a multiringed circus, twelve rings in this gym today. Troy surveyed the action. At one corner ring, pint-size Mites, both boys and girls, sat cross-legged around the ring. In a center ring the Junior purple belts were beginning and there was Darius.

"Jupiter's Eagle, he's first," Troy said. He folded over and pressed his chin to his knees. "Who's doing the music?" All of a sudden he was thinking of all kinds of ways he could have or should have helped Darius prepare for this. Instead, he'd ignored it as much as possible because he thought musical katas were sissy and he didn't want Darius to be candyass.

"Cheney's doing the music," Nick said.

Troy looked down at the table where the microphone was and there was Roger Cheney ready to start the tape. Darius stepped into the ring looking a bit too fresh, Troy thought, with a light blue gi and the purple belt.

"Pluto's helmet," Troy said. "He looks like someone who would do a musical kata." He hated all the color coordinates with gis and belts. In most senses he was not a traditionalist, but he thought a martial artist ought to have either a black gi or a white one. "He's going to embarrass himself." He covered his eyes, but then realized he couldn't see with his eyes covered.

Darius let two phrases of the music play, then he leapt and thrust to the right and almost lost his balance. A sympathetic oooh arose from the stands. Troy groaned. As Darius repeated the movements to the points of the compass, his power, or lack of it, threw him off at each turn until the oohs became titters.

Pluto's helmet, indeed, Troy thought. Pluto's helmet rendered the wearer invisible, and he wished Darius was wearing it.

"What's the music?" he asked.

Keven shrugged.

Nick said, "Shhh."

Troy frowned, trying to place the music. Something from the classical period. Concentrating on the music was a distraction from Darius, flapping around the ring. But even a long kata was only three minutes, so it was soon over. There was a sprinkling of applause. Troy leaned onto his knees and covered his head with his arms.

"Seven-five," said the first judge.

"Seven-five," said the second.

"Seven-six," said the last.

Troy peeked out from under his arm and looked at Keven and Nick. In a range from one to ten, seven-five shouldn't sound like such a bad score, except that even the low scores were usually in the eights. At seven-five, Darius was the winner in musical katas, among all belts in the Junior Division, because his had been the only musical form.

"Well, it was original," Keven said.

"He shouldn't have tried something so complicated," Nick said. "Better to do something simple and do it well."

Troy was thinking Darius shouldn't have tried it at all. Why had Cheney allowed it? Cheney was usually quite blunt about telling you if you weren't ready. Experience, Troy thought, almost hearing Cheney's voice in his ear.

But something about Nick's comment snagged at him. Would Nick really do something easy just to do it well? Darius' kata had been difficult. Done by someone with expertise, it might have been electrifying. If a person only tried simple things, what would he have to test himself against? What would he have to grow toward?

5

*T*here were many styles of karate and some styles adopted their own belt-color systems. In all styles, however, white was the beginning and black the ending. Whether yellow, gray, or purple, the "purple belt" competition, for instance, was for those who'd earned their second belt.

In various rings there were white, purple, blue, green, and brown belts doing forms. Trophies were awarded for first, second, and third for each belt in each division. Some of the Mites had trophies as big as themselves. The brown belts had begun weapons forms, which interested Troy most of all the forms. He was adept at twirling numbchucks and he'd practiced with a staff, but what he really wanted was a samurai sword.

Regularly, someone droned over the loudspeaker, "Will those not taking part in competition in progress please clear the floor." The loudspeaker, the murmur of voices, the muffled stomp of bare feet, and the regular kiais produced a delightful din. When the other belts had finished the form competitions and the floor was cleared for the black belts, there was an unusual quiet. When the black belts were on the floor, there was only one ring in use and every other belt sat and watched in respectful silence.

Even a poorly prepared black belt performed well.

Such precision. Such power. Such balance and speed and grace. The katas, though they displayed the techniques of fighting, did not have to be logical. The techniques could be combined in ways that would not necessarily be effective in defense. As Troy watched, he kept seeing openings for counterblows.

A black belt with a pair of sickles began the weapon competition. There was a stunning whirl of body and blades.

"I'd hate to see a real sickle fight," Darius said, sliding in beside Troy.

For a moment Troy saw the slashed flesh, the kaleidoscope of blood that such a fight would incur. He was glad for the action, so he didn't have to say anything to Darius.

After all the forms, the floor became bedlam again. Participants assumed various positions for warming up and stretching out, in preparation for the fighting competition.

As with the forms, this began with the lower belts. The little ones in the Mite Division lined up by belt, then by height, and were paired two by two. In other divisions, the individuals registered by weight and then lined up along the perimeter of the ring. The referee walked along saying, "You two, you two, you two," in the order in which they stood.

Darius came down onto the floor and stood around with Troy as Troy stretched out, keeping his muscles loose and trying to keep his head loose as well.

"I can't figure out what the judges are doing," Darius said. "They move so fast. I can't make sense of any of the calls."

"Watch ring ten," Troy said. He was irritated with Darius. They did this stuff in class. But if he wanted

Darius to learn, maybe he'd better tell him some things now, while he was paying attention. "There are basically only three calls. Point, no point, and no see." Troy demonstrated the signs for each of the calls.

"No see?" Darius said, laughing as Troy put a forearm across his eyes to signal the call.

"Yes, no see," Troy said. "Look, now." Cheney was judging in ring ten. Cheney called a point and in rapid order the two corner judges extended an open-hand thrust toward the same fighter he had indicated. "That's a point," Troy said. Immediately, the two opponents stood at ready and, on signal from Cheney, began again. "There is a center judge and two corner judges. If two of the three judges agree on a point, the point is given. Look." A corner judge had called a point. The other corner judge pointed to the other contender. The center judge, Cheney, put his arm across his eyes.

"No see?" Darius questioned. "How could he not see? He was on top of them!"

"But the contact was on the other side and he couldn't see who connected with whom. And since the other judges disagree, no point."

Troy slid into his shinpads, boots, gloves, all made out of foam rubber.

"I thought equipment was candyass," Darius said. His tone, Troy noted, was mockingly innocent. Darius knew what they all thought about him doing a musical kata and this was his get-back, Troy realized.

"Boots, gloves, groin cup, and mouthpiece are mandatory," Troy said. Yes, and equipment had once been thought sissy, he acknowledged to himself. But it reduced the chance of injury, which in turn increased training time. "You can gear up like an astronaut these days," he said, nodding toward a man who was putting on kneepads, elbowpads, forearm pads, and head and chest protectors.

The loudspeaker boomed. "Lightweight brown-belt competitors, Junior Division, please assemble at ring ten. Middleweights to ring six. Heavyweights to ring four. This is for Junior Division. All those not involved in current competition please clear the floor."

Troy turned off the announcement after the lightweight information. Ring ten. "Cheney's ring," he said.

"Go get 'em," Darius said.

Darius left the floor and Troy crossed toward ring ten. He let his eyes browse for the two dragoon brown belts. One of them was about his height and weight, a lightweight for sure. The other, Dwight, was quite tall but so thin he was probably also a lightweight. If so, they would probably stand together at ringside and it would be easy enough to push in between them. That way he'd have to draw one or the other.

At ringside, they saved him the trouble. Quite pleased with themselves, they flanked him. He could scarcely keep the grin off his face. He'd love to draw Dwight, he thought. Dwight towered over everyone else and it would look like such an uneven match. What special satisfaction that would be, to cork the tall one. Keven pressed in on the other side of the shorter dragoon. This was not school, Troy thought. He would not get in trouble for smashing one of these guys. His muscles flexed with eagerness as Cheney came along pairing them by twos. It fell into place for both Troy and Keven to be paired with a Dragon. Troy ran his tongue around inside his mouth and refrained from looking at Keven.

This would be the day, he was sure, that he would go further in the eliminations. He had placed fourth twice, but trophies were given just to the top three. This was only his fifth tournament, but there were beginning to be

more in places which were in range for a one-day trip—
Jacksonville, Gainesville, Savannah. There was one in Savannah in four weeks. Karate was an up-and-coming
sport. There was talk about it being included in the
Olympics. His mind floated, dreaming. Perhaps he
would be there! In the meantime, he was hoping to save
ahead to go to some tournaments in Atlanta. That would
require not only entry fee and share of gas money but
meals and motel money as well. Not to mention permission from Mom and Dad.

As the matches in his ring began, he watched with
special care. This was not like sparring at the studio,
where he knew everyone and knew their styles and their
levels of skill. This was the unknown. Except for the ones
he'd observed at other tournaments, he didn't know what
these boys could do. And even with the ones he'd seen
before, he didn't know what progress they had made
since last time.

He studied each participant who might, in just minutes, be his opponent. He watched their stances, noticed
which hand they kept forward, from which side they
threw which technique, and which techniques scored.
He watched to see how they faked and how they responded to a fake. He tried to judge with the judges,
calling the points to himself.

Then Keven was up. Cheney asked for a substitute to
judge the match. A judge never presided when one of his
own students was in the ring. Keven and What's-his-
name, whose name was Stuart, then assumed the ready
stance. As soon as the judge signaled, Keven faked a pull
to the left and came in with a backfist from the right for
the first point. They scrapped a bit, blocking and coun-
tering, before Keven connected with a reverse punch for
the second point.

"Allll right!" Troy shouted. The musketeer was flashy,

49

but flash didn't count if it didn't connect. Had he done a kata? Troy wondered. Flashy counted in the forms. If you were judging by looks and not by what connected, you would think the dragoon was the better fighter. Keven got in with a front leg kick, with plenty of extension, and the match was over. Troy wished he had a stopwatch. Forty-five seconds? Keven bowed and held up his hands. The dragoon bowed and touched gloves with Keven.

"That's what comes of practicing in candlelight," Troy whispered to Dwight as they stepped into the ring. Cheney's substitute stayed in as Troy and Dwight shook hands and took the ready stance. The referee sliced a hand through the air to indicate the onset of the match.

Dwight jabbed air and stepped back. Troy almost laughed. He didn't counter because there was nothing to counter. Dwight jabbed again and Troy leaned away from the jab, then hopped in with a flying sidekick. Dwight stepped away from the kick and countered with a ridgehand that missed. All the missing boiled into frustration and they flew at each other with full contact force. The crowd roared. And the judge roared.

"Break! Too much contact, way too much contact." The boys broke apart immediately and went to neutral corners. Troy was disgusted with himself. He knew better than to lose control. What had made him flare like that? The judge spoke of unsportsmanlike conduct but, since it was both of them, merely issued a warning. Troy still wanted to bust ass, but he reminded himself to keep his control. He tried to dredge up the Positive Mental Attitude from wherever he'd lost it. Dwight's face was raging red and Troy wondered if his own face was as red. He felt the heat of it.

The judge gave the signal to resume and Troy and Dwight circled each other like wary dogs.

"Fight, fight," someone called from the stands.

"Go get 'em, Troy," Keven called.

Troy was aware of the time. If the score was even in two minutes, they would go into overtime. But it was embarrassing to go into overtime zero-zero. He went in with a backknuckle over the top and Dwight came back with an underkick and they both missed again and fury flared. They pummeled and kicked and threw techniques without physical or mental control.

"You're out and you're out!" the judge yelled, pointing first into Troy's face and then into Dwight's. "Timekeeper, both fighters are disqualified for excessive contact."

Troy opened his mouth to say something but the judge had already turned away and summoned the next two competitors into the ring. Troy looked at Cheney, who had stepped back into the ring to resume judging. But Cheney was focusing on the new participants and didn't meet Troy's eye. Being disqualified, especially after a warning, was a terrible and careless thing. Troy was certain that Cheney would have plenty to say about it later.

Nick was by him, touching his shoulder, saying, "It's okay, it's okay. You couldn't help it."

Nick meant to be comforting, but Troy knew there was no excuse for such an outburst.

"At least he didn't beat you," Nick said.

"I beat myself," Troy said, his lips stiff and tight. He had lost control, and didn't know how he'd done it. Control was what karate was all about, having the skills to control yourself in a tight situation, rather than let someone else in the situation control you. He had forgotten how to think, forgotten his PMA. He could hear Cheney now saying, "What you practice is what you do under pressure," but the rage was still in him. Now he

51

not only wanted to beat Dwight but wanted to take on all three of the dragoons and beat them handily. Candlelight indeed!

He and Nick stood near the ring waiting for Keven to come up again. For the moment the loudspeaker person had given up trying to clear the floor. Keven was fighting again. The match went into overtime, two-two. Overtime was a sudden-death match. Whoever got the next point was the winner. Troy hated overtime because it seemed more a matter of luck than skill, although another one of Cheney's sayings was, "The harder I work the luckier I get." Keven's opponent got inside with a backfist and made the winning point. From Troy's gut rose a feeling that surprised him. He was glad Keven had lost.

"Good going," he said, pounding Keven on the back, trying to rid himself of the begrudging feeling. He felt a little unhinged, angry at Keven because Keven had three-pointed a dragoon and he hadn't even one-pointed Dwight. He followed Nick and Keven into the stands and stared without spirit at the beginning of the black-belt fighting.

"Hey, you're not even paying attention," Darius observed.

Troy shrugged.

"Didn't you hear Nick say he'd won four matches?"

Troy shrugged again.

"Didn't you hear Nick say he'd won four matches?" Darius repeated, and poked Troy in the ribs.

"Four? Hey, Nick, that's great," Troy said at last.

6

*F*or the first time ever, Troy dreaded going to karate class. Never mind that Nick said he couldn't help it. Cheney would surely not share that view. At school, he and Dwight had glared at one another. Troy had wanted to spit. He knew that his being disqualified was not Dwight's fault, but he wanted it to be Dwight's fault. He commanded his brain to think of revenges, but his imagination failed him.

In the car on the way to class he was silent. He didn't even tell them it was Turkey Trot Festival in Washington, Indiana. There was a prize for the best-dressed turkey. Well, he'd never win. He wasn't dressed well enough. He waited for Keven or Nick to comment on his silence, and when neither did, he didn't know whether to be grateful or upset. Apparently they, too, were waiting for Cheney's verbal ax to fall on his head.

Darius, surprisingly, was there before them. Not late, but early. A first. After the stretching-out exercises, Cheney called Darius and Troy aside. Troy steeled himself. Apparently Darius was going to hear a few words too, about the poor showing in the kata.

"Troy, I want you to help Darius work on the techniques for his next belt. Darius, you earn that belt by the first of the year. You either work at it and make some progress or you're out, okay?"

Darius nodded and said, "Yes, sir."

"Troy, as his friend, I want you to shepherd him through, okay? That is, if he wants to go."

"I do, sir," Darius replied.

Cheney's tone and the "okays" he inserted softened the remarks but Troy knew that whatever Roger Cheney was going to say to him could not be softened by "okays." Cheney said nothing further, however, but left Darius and Troy and began instructing the others. The silence was worse for Troy than any words Cheney might have said. He swallowed and swallowed and swallowed before he could lessen the lump in his chest enough to begin with Darius.

For each belt, there were certain routines to learn. For blue belt, Darius needed to know the techniques by which you grab your opponent. Cheney had affixed numbers to them, for aid in learning.

"Twelve," Troy called out, to test Darius, to see where he was.

Darius gave Troy a blank look.

Troy let out a huge, breathy, disgusted sigh. "Twelve," he said again, and he proceeded to demonstrate by taking hold of Darius. Darius wasn't so dense that he didn't catch on. When Troy released him, he grabbed Troy likewise.

Troy outlined the blue-belt requirements for Darius, who acted as though he'd never heard them before. With strained patience Troy ran through each one, guiding Darius' practice. He was immensely relieved when Cheney called break.

During break Troy wandered around the studio practicing kicks. He didn't follow Cheney around, exactly, but he wanted Cheney to know he wasn't avoiding him. When Cheney walked into the adjacent office, Troy stood within view of the doorway, kicking and popping the pantleg of his gi. He happened to be looking across the room toward the outside door when, just at the end of break, Dwight and the other two dragoons came into the studio. Troy's eyes popped along with the gi pop. The three incomers slid into chairs by the door.

During the sparring between unequals he was matched with a twelve-year-old white belt. The temptation was almost overwhelming to show off for the dragoons or even to slide into thinking this kid was their proxy. It took his utmost concentration to keep his control and to help the kid practice. When the sparring with equals began, Cheney paired him with Keven, and the dragoons stood up and left. Troy couldn't puzzle that out. He would have thought they would especially want to observe Keven and him together. He and Keven eyed each other and shrugged, and fell into a spirited but good-natured sparring. Troy was relieved to be over the resentment he'd felt toward Keven on Saturday.

After warming down and just before closing meditation, Cheney had some announcements.

"I've had a call from the Crab Creek Campground on Golden Isle," he said. "On October 5, during a camp for children with muscular dystrophy, they want us to give a karate demonstration. That's a Friday and a school holiday. Teachers' workday, or something. Troy, I'd like to ask you to be in charge of working out the demonstration, okay? And, Darius, Keven, Nick, will you help out? How about it, Troy? Gentlemen?"

Troy pulsed with dread and delight. "Yes, sir, if you think I can do it, sir." Immediately he wanted to bite off his words, all but "yes, sir." Of course Cheney thought he could do it, or he wouldn't have asked. The others nodded confirmation and Troy wished he'd been more confident.

"And I am pleased to announce the scheduling of the

black-belt test for Nick and Keven for next Monday," Cheney said. A chorus of congratulatory cries went up. Troy's emotions, already mixed, had risen at the words "black-belt test," then crashed at the omission of his own name. He felt a shadow cross his face and he saw Cheney notice it. Cheney led them into the meditation and, at the end, walked past Troy, heading for the office.

"Embrace it, Troy," Cheney said as he passed. And that was all. Embrace it, Troy. Troy knew what Cheney meant. Hold it close and learn from it. But he'd embraced it since Saturday and he didn't think he should be punished for it. Everyone made mistakes—didn't Cheney know that? He wanted to go after Cheney and tell him but he knew the more he said the worse he would make it for himself. He turned and followed the others to the door.

"Coming for pizza?" Keven was asking Darius. Nick, Keven, and Troy almost always went for pizza after class.

"I'm not going," Troy said. "I'm going home." He wasn't going to ask for a ride. The studio was six miles from home, out by the junior college, but he'd walk. He probably even needed that. "I'll walk," he said.

"My dad's here," Darius said. "We'll take Troy home."

"Why don't we just go to your house for a while," Keven said to Troy. "Okay?"

Troy shrugged and nodded, eased a little by the attention of his friends.

"You don't mind, do you, Dad?" Keven asked Nick.

Nick tilted his head and held one hand up. "My pizza grubbers have just abandoned me," he said to Darius' father, who had stepped out of the car. "Can I interest you in joining me for a pizza after one of us takes the three of them to Troy's?"

"Why not," he said.

All three boys piled in with Darius' father, who drove them to Troy's.

"Did you see them? Did you see them come to gloat?" Troy said as the three boys walked up the sidewalk to his house. "Did you see them come to our studio and sit there? They sat there like goons. Did you see it?"

"Cool down, Troy," Darius said.

"You shut up," Troy said.

"Let him get the venom out," Keven said.

Venom! He felt like striking Keven with his fangs. What did Keven know about it, anyway? Keven didn't understand anything. Vengeance is what he had, not venom. He pushed open the front door and Darius and Keven followed him in. All three spoke politely to Troy's parents as they passed through the living room. In Troy's room there was barely a place to stand, much less sit.

"Close your eyes for three minutes," Troy said, shutting the door and motioning them back against it. Darius and Keven closed their eyes and Troy attacked the morass of mess. He picked up the newest layer, which consisted of schoolbooks, clothes that could be worn again, and current drawing projects. He hung the clothes on pegs in his closet. The other things he stacked at the side of the drawing board, the only surface he invariably kept clear. In several swoops he picked up the other stuff—clothes, gis, gloves, boots, magazines, assorted papers that might or might not be trash, and threw them up onto the beds that traversed the closets. Then he pulled the short curtains across the bed area.

"I never saw that curtain drawn before," Darius said.

"You're supposed to have your eyes closed," Troy said.

Darius reclosed his eyes. "Your three minutes are up," he said.

"Okay, you can open them now," Troy said.

Keven, who'd been standing with his eyes open, said, "Hey. Looks like your mother cleaned your room."

"No," Troy said. "All my good junk is still here." He indicated the mess behind the curtain.

Keven laughed and nodded in appreciation. His mother was always straightening up his room and throwing out things he considered important. "But where are you going to sleep?"

"I'll go off that bridge when I come to it," Troy said.

Darius had turned the desk chair and straddled it backward. Keven took the spare chair and sat down the normal way but slouched until he was barely making contact with the seat bottom. Troy leaned against a closet door.

"I want to get those candyass dragoons," Troy said.

"We figured that out," Darius said.

"Why did they come to our studio?" Keven asked.

"I can answer that in one word," Troy said. "Aggravation."

"Are they trying to start something?" Keven asked.

"Gee, Kev, you catch on quick," Troy said.

"Let's give them what they're looking for," Keven said.

"Count me out," said Darius.

"Oh, come off it, Darius," Troy said. "You act like we've killed seven people today, and it's really only six." He backed up and perched on the bottom rung of the bunk ladder, and as though the movement itself had nudged his brain, he had an idea. "Hey, what about that fluorescent sign in front of their studio?"

"What about it?" Keven asked.

"Let's play anagrams."

"Yeah, yeah," Darius said immediately.

"What's anagrams?" Keven asked.

"Shoe. Fuse. Snag," Darius said, already beginning. "Heat, heart, soup," he reeled off, using the letters from

58

the sign: "HOUSE OF DRAGONS: THE COMPLETE MAR-TIAL ARTS."

"'Soup, oh sure,'" Keven said as Troy explained anagrams.

It was the name House of Dragons that had drawn Troy to it almost three years ago. It sounded so fierce and official. A karate studio called House of Dragons just had to be better than one called Cheney's Karate Studio. Or so he had thought when he started. And so the dragoons still thought.

"We can get 'oh sure,'" Darius was saying. "Or 'assure.'"

"'Ass, oh sure,'" Troy said. "Let's get 'candyass' in there."

"There's no Y," Darius pointed out.

"Hey, candleass," Troy said. "Can we get 'candleass'?"

Darius had unstraddled the chair and moved to the drawing board and written the words of the sign on one of the ever-ready sheets of paper. "Yeah, yeah. One candleass coming up," he said, writing the word and penning a slashmark through those letters in what the sign said.

"Candleass Dragoons," Troy said. Thoughts of vengeance were sweet, and his mood was growing sweeter by the minute.

"You've used the only N in 'candleass,'" Darius said.

"'Dragoos,'" Keven said.

Troy and Darius frowned at Keven. "Keven, sometimes I worry about where you park your brains," Troy said.

"'Dragoos,'" Keven said again. "'Gooey'" sort of goes with 'candyass,' I thought."

Troy frowned again. Keven was too slow to see they'd gotten off "candyass" and onto "candleass." But while he

59

frowned, the word "dragoos" rolled around in his head and he began to like it. "Sorry, Kev. On second thought, 'dragoos' sounds just right. Real candleass."

The three of them bent over the paper, looking to see what letters were left.

"'Riot' something," Darius suggested.

"'Forsooth,'" offered Troy.

"'Home of the candleass dragoos,'" said Keven.

"Yeah, yeah," Darius said, scanning the letters and seeing they could get "Home of the" from what was left.

"Let's go do it!" Keven urged, pounding Troy and Darius on the shoulders.

"Not so fast, speedster," Troy said. "Sit down." Keven sat. "We have to consider the letters carefully and plan how to move them in the least amount of time."

Darius was still leaning over the paper, writing down the unused letters in alphabetical order. AEILMPRRT-TTU. "'Ultimate,'" he said. "How about 'Home of the Ultimate Candleass Dragoos'?" Troy and Keven whooped and sparred about the room.

"How about holding it down to a dull roar?" Dad called through the door, and the boys whooped more.

"Okay, plans," Troy said. "Settle down, settle down. Darius, what's the best plan?" He sat by Darius, who was standing at the drawing board.

"Okay. We'll have four unused letters. Keven, you take them off the board." On a fresh piece of paper Darius wrote out the words of the sign again and circled the P, two R's, and a T and handed the paper to Keven. "You get these out of the way." Then he pointed out the most efficient way to change the sign and who was to take down which letters. "Be ready to hand me what I ask for as quickly as possible. Got it?"

They went over it all again in a rehearsal, then left the

room. Troy's mother was in the living room and looked up at the boys.

"We're going to the Quick Stop for Cokes," Troy said. "Want one?"

"No thanks," she said. "You boys behave yourselves."

"Mo-om," Troy said, wondering why she'd said that. She never said that. His parents simply assumed he would behave himself. Had she had a psychic flash? "We allllways behave, right, boys?"

Keven and Darius confirmed their model behavior.

Because they loved the river, they walked two blocks out of the way to walk along it. The House of Dragons was on King Street, two blocks north of Grand Square.

"I wonder if the Altamaha-ha is a night creature as well as a day creature?" Troy mused as they reached the river. His eyes traced the smooth skin of the water.

"You ought to know," Keven said.

"Well, I've only just met her," Troy said, surprised to realize he was making an allegory for Liesl as he spoke. "You don't know everything about someone when you've just met them."

"Well, she's a night creature," Darius said. "There she is now." Darius nodded toward the river.

"Yup, there she is," Troy said. He spoke softly, as if in awe, as if not to frighten the creature away. He was pleased that Darius could see her. Most of the body was just below the surface of the water, her curves making ripples as she glided along upstream, keeping abreast of them. About five feet of her was lifted gracefully, wavering above the water, the magnificent pop eyes watching them even as they watched her.

"I'm going to barf, man," Keven said, frowning.

"You have to have vision, Kev," Troy said.

"Or a few loose screws."

"Come on, Keven. We wouldn't have the space program today if the Wright Brothers hadn't been able to see something that wasn't really there."

"I suppose that sea monster is going to take off and fly," Keven said.

"She might," Troy said.

"If we wanted her to," Darius added.

"*Your* imagination has nothing to do with the space program," Keven said. "That Altamaha-ha has nothing to do with anything."

Troy almost laughed because Keven was pointing to the Ha-ha even in the midst of his denials. "If we didn't have Altamaha-has and unicorns and dreams of flying we'd never come up with new things," he said. "Such as airplanes and computers. Or the cure for cancer. Sometimes imagination stretches into reality."

"Like moog synthesizers and things to play on it," Darius said. "Gee, Troy. That's profound. It really is."

"Profound? Really?" Troy said.

"What's profound?" Keven asked.

"Oops, there she goes," Troy said, looking at the river. "Keven's chased her away with skepticism."

"Or the cure for muscular dystrophy," Darius said.

"What is muscular dystrophy, anyway?" Troy asked.

"Why didn't you ask Cheney?" Keven asked.

"There were some tense moments there, in case you didn't notice," Troy said.

"Deterioration of the muscles," Darius said. "You know, Jerry's kids."

"Whose kids?"

"Jerry Lewis. The telethons."

"Juno's peacock!"

"Well, it's not the kids' fault that Jerry parades them across the stage of America. The kids are probably thrilled to be on television, just as we would be."

"Minerva's owl!" Troy said. He saw some of the children in his mind's eye and felt inadequate for the assignment.

"Would you quit that," Keven said.

"Quit what?" Troy asked in return.

"All that Minerva, Juno, Jupiter stuff. I don't even know what you're talking about."

"Is it my fault you don't know your mythology?"

"How could he have earned so much money for the cause without calling attention to it?" Darius said, ignoring the interruption.

"Cheney should have put you in charge," Troy said.

"Well, I'd do very well with the kids," Darius said, "but it wouldn't be much of a karate demonstration."

"That's for sure," Troy and Keven said in chorus, and they all laughed.

"I might try a sweep kick to the chest," Darius said.

Troy nodded. "That's about your style," he said. A sweep kick was at ground level, sweeping a foot behind an opponent's foot in a tripping motion. It wasn't even a good technique on its own, without follow-up techniques. Sort of like a Q without a U, he thought.

They had crossed the ends of Princess, Queen, and Prince as they walked along. Now they were at the end of the cross street which would take them over to the House of Dragons on King Street. Streetlights glowed eerily through tree limbs and filtered unevenly onto rooftops, parked cars, and sidewalks.

"Step in the light and you're not too bright," Keven said, slinking along in the shadows.

"Yeah, yeah, but there are no shadows in King Street," Darius said.

"And you keep walking like that and you'll attract attention for sure," Troy said.

"Yeah, act normal," Darius said.

"Don't ask the impossible," Troy said.

Keven still walked in the shadows and, as they approached the corner of King Street, said, "I'll be the lookout." He walked beside the concrete apron of the once service station, now karate studio. He stood on the corner, as though waiting to cross the street, and motioned an all-clear to Darius and Troy.

"I never thought about that," Darius said as he and Troy met Keven at the lighted sign freestanding where the gas pumps used to be. "I never thought about being so visible, about anyone coming along being able to see us."

"Are you scared?" Troy asked.

"Of course I'm scared. I'm not stupid."

"It's just a prank," Keven said.

"I know it's just a prank," Darius said. Keven had plucked away the unneeded letters and Darius' nimble fingers began the rearranging. "I know it's just a prank," Darius said again. "Otherwise I wouldn't be here. We're not going to damage anybody or anything."

"Except a few egos," Troy said, handing Darius an M to change "House" to "Home."

"Guess what, friends," Keven said. "This sign has two sides."

Troy groaned. "I knew that. Why didn't I think of that? We can't take time for both sides."

Darius asked for letters and held out his hand for them much as a surgeon asks for and holds out a hand for scalpel and clamps.

"A car just turned from Grand Square," Keven said.

"Quick," Troy said, flustered that he hadn't also considered this possibility. But his friends were quick. Keven came at him with sparring techniques while Darius stood casually in front of the sign.

The car passed and Darius said, "Dragoos," and he was quickly handed the R-A-G-O-O-S. "The D, the D," he said. Keven and Troy looked at one another, shrugged, and Keven stepped to the other side of the sign and handed Darius the needed D.

"It's beautiful," Troy said, stepping back to look. Darius had not stepped back for an admiring glance but had moved to the other side of the sign, lifting letters off. "No," Troy said when he saw what Darius was doing. "One side is enough. Let's go!" His adrenaline had given him a shot of alarm. "Come on," he said, taking a few steps toward the side street. "We're going to be caught." Cheney wouldn't like what they were doing, and Troy would never get his black belt. When they didn't follow, he flung his hands in agitation and returned to the sign where Darius had retrieved the borrowed D so he could make "Candleass" and compensated by simply leaving "Dragoos" short one letter, which struck them as especially funny. They darted, giggling, down the darkened side street, constantly glancing back as though they were being chased. After they turned one corner, however, they gave in to the giddiness of the adventure and the way the sign had turned out and laughed all the way to the Quick Stop, where they bought Cokes.

Back down on King Street, shining into the Hanover night, was the sign "HOME OF THE ULTIMATE CAN- DLEASS RAGOOS."

7

*S*choolbooks and drawings for the newspaper in hand, Troy took an early-morning walk along the river and into the empty town. Mr. Hutton had made some suggestions for a revision of the courthouse sketch and Troy had taken advantage of it to make some squiggles indicating people on the walkway and on the stairs. No one but him would know that two certain figures represented him and Liesl and the day he followed her across Grand Square. Thoughts of Liesl made him smile. Thoughts of "ragoos" made him laugh.

Mr. Hutton's car was at the curb in front of the *Historian,* but Troy knew it would be moved before time for customers of the shops to need the space. As he opened the door to the newspaper office a string of bells tied to the inside handle signaled his arrival. He called out to announce himself and crossed to Mr. Hutton's private office.

"Come in, come in," the dark-haired editor said.

Troy took two steps and set the drawings on the cluttered desk.

"Good, good, this is very good," Mr. Hutton said as he looked at the drawings. "Yes, this is perfect. Great idea, Troy, putting people in the picture. Makes it look alive."

"Thanks. That's me right there." He pointed to a certain squiggle.

"Oh, really? I'm glad you pointed it out," said Mr. Hutton. "I didn't recognize you. Who's that with you?"

"Uh, well," Troy said, surprised by the editor's participation in the fantasy, "I guess it's you, sir."

"No, no, he's not tall enough," Mr. Hutton said. The man leaned back in his chair, stretched his arms out, then folded them behind his head. "Any news out there? It's been a dead week."

Troy bit his lip, thinking about "Ragoos." He'd give a lot to see a picture of that sign on the photo page of the *Historian*. But he wouldn't give enough to give himself away, he decided. "No, sir," he said. "I don't know a thing."

"Well, get out there and make some news," Mr. Hutton said.

Out on Princess Avenue Troy had Liesl on his mind again. A week ago this very morning she was actually on the sidewalk with him. He shook his head and called himself crazy. He'd seen her every school morning since, and always with Donnie Duggan. Who did he think he was fooling? Liesl and Donnie went together, that was obvious. There was no room for him.

In front of the old Ritz he gave a front jab and a front kick toward the faded lobby card of Clark Gable and Vivien Leigh. His hand and foot brushed the glass like a whisper. Gable didn't even blink.

"Well, you didn't make me blink, either," he said aloud to the picture, which was a permanent fixture at the defunct theater. "I thought your movie was boring." He darted out with a sidekick and the tip of his grungy shoe pecked a hole in the glass.

He gasped, planted his foot back on the sidewalk, and looked around to see if anyone had seen. The morning street was empty. He put his hand to the glass, to cover the damage, or heal it. His kick had been so swift there

67

hadn't even been a shattering sound, just a quick, muffled sort of chunk.

"Bellerophon's horse!" he said. He had recently learned how to rewire a dimmer switch, and now, he guessed, he'd learn how to replace a pane of glass. Inside his head he saw dollar bills which could be better spent for karate things. He looked around again, prepared to meet the accusing eye of some early shopowner. Still, there was no one. No one would know who broke the glass and, more probably, no one would even notice it was broken. He shrugged and walked casually along toward school.

In front of his homeroom, Keven accosted him.

"They're looking for you," Keven said. "They're really laying for you."

"Who?" Troy asked, to tease Keven. He knew very well "who."

"The ragoos, man. The ragoos. The sign."

"Oh, yeah, the ragoos," Troy said. "The sign. So, why are they looking for me?"

"They know you did it," Keven said. "We'll have to stick together. You don't need all three of them jumping you."

"I'd relish it," Troy said, and as he said it he saw the fierce Dragons coming up the hall. Just as he noticed them, Liesl spoke from his left flank.

"Whose birthday is it today?" she asked.

Before he could say, "Samuel Johnson, English author and lexicographer," the Dragons had pushed up around him and left Keven and Liesl outside the cozy ring.

"You are the candleass," Dwight said.

"And what do you mean, Ragoo?" Bert asked.

Their maneuver had drawn his attention for only a moment, but when he looked back at Liesl, she was gone. His temper flared. How dare they block him off from Liesl? Just as quickly as he fired up, he cooled down. He wasn't about to let them know they bothered him.

"Say, I'll bet you want me for your team in the Beach Volleyball Championships," he said. He reached outside their circle and quickly drew Keven in. "I'm really sorry, but you're too late. It's for two-man teams, you know, and Keven and I have already teamed up. In fact, we're catching a plane to Hartford in just a few minutes."

"You two don't scare us," said Stuart, whom Keven had soundly beaten in the tournament.

"Oh, I know," Troy said, turning "know" into a two-syllable word. "I can tell by the way your hair curls that you're fearless." He also knew they weren't unwise enough to trounce him here at school in front of his homeroom.

"How come you messed with our sign?" Dwight said. "We're going to shove a candle up your—" The bell interrupted, indicating the beginning of homeroom.

"Sorry," Troy said, shoving Keven ahead of him, out of the fold, and into the art class. "We don't want to be unpunctual."

"Thought you had a plane to catch, huh?" Bert said. "What about the plane?"

They heard Dwight say, "Don't be stupid, huh? Just don't be stupid," and they hooted with laughter.

"Unpunctual?" Keven said. "You have made me unpunctual." He scooted out the door and down the hall to his own homeroom.

All day the ragoos lurked. They popped out from hallways, doorways, and from behind fellow students. "We'll get your candleass," they said to Troy all day long.

"I just can't wait until they try," Keven said. "Just let them start it, that's all I'm waiting for."

"Count me out," Darius said.

69

"Yeah, yeah," Troy said. "I heard you before you said it."

Except from the ragoos there was no mention of the sign. Apparently some late or early Dragon had passed by and reconstituted the sign before anyone else saw it. Troy was disappointed. It was like trying to make thunder and making only a thud.

On both Wednesday and Thursday Troy arrived at school early and stood in the hall outside his homeroom. He was armed with birthdays—Scotch orator Henry Brougham; Charles Carroll, American revolutionary leader; American novelist Upton Sinclair—but Liesl didn't come along. He even sidled down the hall looking into the rooms nearby, but he didn't see her. Had she come along just looking for him the other day? His heart leapt at the thought. If so, why didn't she come by again? Was it because he hadn't responded? Those damn dragoons! He looked for her in the lunchroom, ready to announce the birthdays, but he didn't see her anywhere. Charles Carroll, he was ready to tell her, was the last surviving signer of the Declaration of Independence.

During those days, the ragoos continued to appear in verbal ambush from unexpected places, until it became expected. They seemed to be watching him closely enough to learn his schedule and appear, always all three together, before and after every class.

"They're working up to something," Keven said.

"I think it's pretty comical myself," Troy said.

Except for Upton Sinclair's birthday, which wasn't all that exciting, the calendar for September 20 was unusually dull. He had nothing clever to announce to Nick on the way to karate class. Once there, however, the door to the studio had its own announcement. There were words printed on the door in mustard-yellow, highway-department-color paint: "NASTYASS. YOU'LL GET YOURS."

"Zeus!" Troy said. "They have no imagination."

"What do you know about it?" Nick asked.

"The ragoos," Troy said, then caught himself. "It has to be those dragoons."

"Who?" Nick asked.

"You know, Dad," Keven said. "Those guys from the House of Dragons."

"Well," Nick said. "They'll get theirs."

Inside, when they were in their places, Cheney entered and stopped them mid-bow.

"Before we begin, I have an item of business. Perhaps you noticed the new sign on the door." He paused while everyone acknowledged they had noticed. "There is no doubt in my mind that our new sign is in exchange for someone else's new sign." Heads turned. There were puzzled murmurs. "There is also little doubt in my mind who is responsible for initiating this trade-off, but I would prefer for the artisan to identify himself."

How had Cheney found out? Troy wondered. Had the dragoons yapped to Cheney, or did their instructor call Cheney? If Cheney was pretty sure he'd done it, Troy knew he would only be in worse trouble by denying it. Besides, it occurred to him that he'd given himself away to Nick by using the term "ragoos." If Nick and Cheney talked, the perpetrator of the prank would be confirmed.

Knowing his black belt would vanish further into the distance, Troy dropped his head and raised his hand.

"Thank you, Troy," Cheney said. "Did you manage this project on your own or did you have assistance?"

Head still down, hand still up, Troy made no other move.

"I helped, sir," Darius said. Troy looked up then, and

71

saw Darius ahead of him, holding up a hand. The Hand Also Riseth, Troy thought, not amused at his pun.

"Anyone else?" Cheney asked.

Troy kept himself from looking sideways at Keven. Everyone knew that the three of them were friends. But Keven did not speak up or indicate his involvement in any way. Troy wondered what Nick thought, what he would say.

"All right, Troy, Darius," Cheney said. He pulled a twenty-dollar bill from his pocket. "Here's money, which you will owe me. Walk over to K-Mart and buy whatever you need to restore the door. I don't think one coat of repainting will cover the marvelous brilliance of the color."

Troy moved through the ranks to take the bill and Darius joined him.

"Gentlemen," Cheney said to them, and he bowed. They returned the bow and as they walked away Cheney faced the others, exchanged bows, and began the meditation.

They bought a half-gallon of light green paint, as close to the present door color as they could estimate.

"Two brushes?" Troy asked Darius.

"We'll be painting each other if we both paint at once," Darius said. They bought one brush and trudged back to the studio.

Neither of them mentioned Keven's abstention. They both understood it, Troy guessed. Not only had Keven seen his black belt fading into the background but he'd seen his father looming in the foreground. But now Keven was in double trouble, Troy thought, because Nick knew. Nick knew that where go Troy and Darius, there also goes Keven. If Troy was glad about any of this, it was that he'd already scotched the scheduling of his black-belt test so he hadn't been tempted to deny the truth.

As Darius began painting, Troy read from the label. "'Wait at least twelve hours before applying second coat.'"

"And it'll take three coats, for sure," Darius said. The words he'd painted over were still clearly visible, though chartreuse now instead of mustard.

"Shall we stick together on the future coats or draw straws?" Troy asked.

"You can have tomorrow," Darius said, handing Troy the brush. "I'll take Saturday."

Troy began painting and realized that Darius had painted the easiest part.

In the morning he decided he'd rather paint the second coat before school than after, if the door was dry. It wasn't quite twelve hours but perhaps it was close enough. He dragged his old bicycle out of the garage to ride the six miles.

"Where in the world are you going?" Mother called out a window as he checked the tires.

"I have to run out to the studio for something," he said. He had hoped to get the bike and be gone without them noticing, but Mother seemed to notice everything. Dad noticed only what he saw through a camera lens.

"Well, for heaven's sake, I'll be glad to take you."

"Nah," he said. "Thanks just the same."

He didn't ride his bike much anymore and was a bit surprised at the pleasure he found in the stretch and push of his legs. The pressure of his feet against the pedals made him smile. He liked the feel of his muscles in motion.

At the studio the brush, paint, and mineral spirits and newspapers were behind the shrubbery where they'd left them. Thank goodness it hadn't rained, he thought. He touched a finger to the door. Dry. Not even tacky. He pried open the lid of the paint can and as he dipped and brushed he fancied painting stylized karate figures sparring around the door. He reminded himself to stick to the project at hand.

The second coat dimmed the lettering to unreadable streaks. The third coat would do it. The job took him twenty minutes and the slap-slap cleaning of the brush took him almost as long. Cleaning the brush, he thought, was nastyass. The work made him think of the broken display glass at the Ritz and he knew he'd have to fix it even though no one had noticed. Otherwise, he'd be like Keven, and for less reason.

On the ride back to school he invented a series of confrontations with the ragoos. What he and Keven and Darius had done to the sign at the House of Dragons was just a prank. They caused no damage and restoring the sign took only a little time. What the ragoos had done in return was vandalism. They had defaced property and the restoration cost time and money. My time and my money, he thought, and the more he thought about it, the madder he got. One at a time he would sidekick the three of them to kingdom come. The distant waving of a black belt did not interfere with his fantasy.

As he was locking the bike to the bike rack someone spoke.

"Whose birthday is it today?"

Troy looked up and there was Liesl with Donnie Duggan. Habitually, he kept several days ahead on the calendar but his brain would bring forth nothing for this day. Liesl and Donnie walked on, leaving him there with his blank mind. His recent scenarios with the ragoos played across his senses and filled the space. But there, inside his skull, was Liesl, watching his heroics. In the picture she did not clap and cheer. She turned away.

He stomped his foot in frustration, as he had on the sidewalk behind her that first day. She liked him. She must. The other morning she went out of her way to speak to him. And just now she spoke even though she was with Donnie. He coveted the afterimage of her hugging her schoolbooks and saying, "Whose birthday is it today?" And whose birthday was it? he wondered. And what would he do now if the dragoons attacked? Even if she didn't witness it, the word would circulate.

Now the waving black belt caught his attention. From somewhere behind Troy's eyeballs, a miniature Cheney was waving semaphore signals. A true martial artist does not seek confrontation and skillfully avoids it whenever possible. A martial artist thinks his way out of situations. Cheney said these words constantly. Though he trained them thoroughly for self-defense, Cheney said the bash-bam-boom of the martial-arts movies was pure entertainment.

Troy entered the building warily, hoping he would not run into any ragoos until he had decided how he might defuse them without a blow.

His watchfulness was wasted. All three ragoos were mysteriously absent from school.

That night after supper Troy tried to find Liesl's phone number. He wanted to call her and tell her it was H. G. Wells' birthday, Cheese and Butter Festival in Denmark, and Moon Cake Festival in Singapore. There were no Trunzos in the phone book.

8

The sun was just rising behind him as Troy met Keven and Darius at the river. They were going to work out some routines for the demonstration for the muscular-dystrophy kids. In that standstill between the incoming and outgoing tide, the river was a vast reflecting pool. As they began to throw techniques, the shadows of their kicks and punches darted out over the water.

"Where's Nick?" Troy asked.

Keven shrugged. "He had to work a little while this morning. Then we're going fishing for the weekend."

Had Nick asked Keven if he was involved in the sign fiasco? Troy wondered. What had Keven said? Was there something fishy here more than going fishing? Nick never worked on Saturdays. Why wasn't he here at practice?

"They're holding the Pennsylvania Bedmaking Championships in Philadelphia today," Troy said, to bury his thoughts.

"Whoopdeedoo," Keven said, kicking to within a hairbreadth of Troy's left ear. Troy brought his hands up underneath the kick and Keven hopped backward to keep from being toppled.

"It's also the birthday of the ice-cream cone," Troy said, spinning Keven by the shoulder and giving him a pseudo punch in the jaw. Watching the motions transfer to the water made Troy think of Liesl dancing to her reflection in the storefront window. At the thought of her, his mind cast her image onto the water so she was mirrored there beside him.

"Hey, look at that," Darius shouted as the shadow of one of his kicks extended twenty feet across the water.

"In a minute you'll be clipping the sea monster in the chin," Troy said, twirling, twirling, perfecting his spinning kick.

"Yeah, man, sure," Keven said. "Sea monster, sure."

"You haven't seen it yet, have you?" Troy said.

"Don't waste my time," Keven said.

"Look, there she is now," Troy said, pointing to the river. "Where do you suppose deep ripples come from on a still day like this?" An actual swell, like the wake from a boat, moved in rows toward either shore.

Keven followed the V-line of the swell, looking for a boat. Then he made a thrust at Darius. Darius blocked and threw a reverse punch which Keven blocked and countered with a front leg kick which clipped Darius in the chest.

"Don't you have any imagination?" Troy asked. "Look. There. She's just surfaced."

In spite of themselves, both Keven and Darius looked.

"You missed her," Troy said. "I think she's shy."

"Look over there," Darius said. "It's resurfaced. Gee, golly, gosh! It's a hundred feet long."

"No, no, only forty," Troy corrected. "You have to make it believable."

"Okay, okay, I see it," Keven said. "Now let's get back to practicing. I want to practice for my test."

"Hey, man," Troy said, mocking Keven's most used phrase. "What do you think this is, your own private black-belt-test practice? We're here to work out a routine for the muscular-dystrophy kids, remember?"

"I just can't think about anything but the test, man," Keven said.

"Well, try, man, try," Troy said. He couldn't think about much else himself, and the fact that he wouldn't be taking it. But he was willing to try to obliterate the whole thing.

"I don't think those kids would even want to see a karate demonstration," Keven said. "I mean if I was a kid and was losing my muscles, I don't think I'd want to see anybody showing off with theirs."

Troy nodded. Keven's thoughts were identical to his own. Perhaps he should talk to Cheney about it.

"Come on, you guys, where is your head?" Darius said. "I sing, right? If something happened to my vocal cords, do you think I'd never want to hear anyone sing again? I think I would appreciate vocal music all the more."

"Yeah, yeah," Troy said, mimicking Darius' favorite phrase now. He nodded, now, at Darius, relieved with the good sense of his example.

"I don't know, man," Keven said.

"Well, I have to do it," Troy said. "Are you in or out?"

"I'm in," Keven said.

"I think it would be good to simulate what we do in class," Troy said. "We can begin with meditation and the explanation for bowing. Then we'll do some stretching exercises and some sparring. Maybe we can work out a humorous sketch with the sparring."

"With you as hero, no doubt," Keven said.

"No, as a matter of fact I thought we'd let Darius be the hero," Troy said. As a matter of fact, he hadn't thought about it at all. "The humble purple belt whipping up on the haughty brown belts." Now he nodded at himself. He would reverse the sparring order and have the sparring with equals first. He and Keven would go at

78

it, showing off skill and speed, then during the sparring between unequals, Darius would cork them both.

"Black belt," Keven said. "I'll be a black belt."

Troy could have done without the reminder.

"Probably," Keven said, tacking the word on for humility's sake, Troy guessed. "We have to work Dad's part in."

Nick should have been here, Troy thought, smacking a forearm into his hand. He and Keven had played around with one another so much, as conqueror and conquered, that working out their part of the routine was easy. They were expert at making well-choreographed dramatic punches and falls. The hard part was inventing the absent Nick and responding to Darius' poor techniques.

"Since you're going to be the big black belt," Troy said to Keven, "you are going to be the most supercilious."

"What?" Keven asked.

"Supercilious," Darius put in. "Don't you know A. A. Milne's poem 'King John's Christmas,' where the people of the town gave him a supercilious stare and passed with noses in the air?"

"No," Keven said. "I don't. At least you have the 'super' part right."

"I'll come after you and we'll be pretty equal at first," Troy said, "then I'll begin to get you."

"You'll love that, won't you?" Keven said.

Troy shrugged. "I think your guilty conscience is getting to you."

"Guilty conscience? For what? For what?" Keven said loudly.

Troy could see that Keven wished to swallow the words as soon as they were out. He clapped Keven on the shoulder reassuringly. "Nothing, nothing. It's okay. I'm sorry I said it."

"It wasn't my idea to mess with their sign," Keven said.

"People go to prison for being accomplices," Darius said.

Troy looked at Darius, surprised at such a remark coming from Darius the peaceable.

"Yeah, yeah," Darius said, smiling only half a smile. "I do want a tiny bit of gratitude. That door is a botch."

"That's good, Darius. That's really good," Troy said.

"I know, I know," Keven said. "I'm a son of a botch. Here's gratitude." Keven bowed deeply to Darius and Troy.

"Now get on with it, Darius," Troy said. "I might just demote you to white belt so I can tell them that a white belt is the most dangerous because he has no control. Then you can come on and take both of us, as planned." They worked on it bit by bit, mugging and modifying, discussing Nick's role as victor and victim as they went along. Darius eventually wiped them out.

"Having a white belt cork us will give a false impression of karate," Keven said.

"You're such a purist," Darius said, playfully cuffing Keven on the chin.

"So I'll tell them that this is a skit we provided for entertainment and then we'll show them what would really happen." Keven and Darius immediately began the routine. Darius came at Troy with a backfist and Troy handily countered and decked him. Then Troy went at Keven and Keven keeled Troy.

"What about Dad?" Keven said.

"We'll work him in," Troy said. "We've already talked about that." He struggled with his feelings for a moment. Keven was being so defensive and it was hard not to be defensive in return. He was the one who wasn't allowed

80

to take the black-belt test. They punched and kicked and countered their way through the routine again. Each fall became grander than the one before. Keven, as the bully being beaten, "oofed" loudly at every blow and clutched himself and whirled in agony before he fell. Finally they were a tangle of pseudo-fractured limbs and laughter. Keven crawled away in retreat. Still belly-down, he cupped his chin in his hands and stared out at the river.

"What are you doing now?" Troy asked.

"I'm looking for sea monsters," Keven said. "While I have my imagination going, I might as well make use of it."

"I told you she was shy," Troy said.

"Well, if she surfaces for you she'll surface for me," Keven said.

Troy pursed his lips and nodded and joined Keven in staring out onto the water. Darius matched Keven's belly-down position and also stared.

"Is this a supercilious stare?" Keven asked.

Troy and Darius exchanged glances and smiled.

There were no ripples now, no sign even of mullet, much less monsters. The white sheen of sun had risen and removed their shadows from the river. In fact, Troy noticed that his shadow had disappeared beneath him as though absorbed into himself. Liesl danced into his mind and he watched the way her hair swayed behind her. After a while he spoke softly, the words barely making it out onto the air.

"I know how you feel about Molly," he said to Darius. He plucked at one of the sparse clumps of grass. "There's this girl I've seen."

"Now I'm going to barf," Keven said.

"Do you talk to her?" Darius asked. "Have you called her?"

81

"I don't even know how to talk to her," Troy said.

"You?" Keven said. "You? The great mouth of the Western world? You just open your mouth and speak, man. Even I know that. If you put your foot in your mouth you spit it out and keep talking. Right, Darius?"

Darius laughed.

"What's it like? How does it feel?" Troy asked. "Liking a girl and having her like you back?"

The three of them continued to stare out over the mirrored water. Wisps of marsh grass began to drift seaward, marking the change of tide.

"Wonderful," Darius said at last. "Fun. Scary."

Troy watched a grasshopper riding one sheaf of marsh grass and wondered what the insect knew or thought about the journey. Did it know it was heading out to sea?

"Scary?" Keven asked. "What's scary?"

"Oh, the putting of foot in mouth," Darius said. "And . . ." He paused again. "Growing up, I guess. Having all these adult feelings when I don't feel very adult most of the time."

"Well, hey, man. Romeo was doing it at our age, so what's the big deal?"

"I don't think of Molly that way," Darius said.

"Liar," Keven said, and the sound of a car approaching ended the conversation. "There's Dad," Keven said, rolling to a sitting position.

The Mercedes pulled to a stop near them on the scrubby dirt lane between River Street and the river. "How's it going?" Nick called out.

"Good, good," Troy said, and the three boys walked to the car, babbling about the routine and how they were going to take Nick out.

Keven climbed into the car. "See you Monday," he said, reminding Troy of what Monday was.

82

"See you," he managed to say. Not only were Keven and Nick taking the black-belt test on Monday but right now they were leaving for a weekend fishing trip. He shoved his hands into his pockets.

"What are you going to do now?" Darius asked.

"Go eat an ice-cream cone," Troy said.

"That figures."

"What are you going to do?"

"Call Molly."

"That figures."

They dusted off their clothes and walked to River Street and split, Darius heading for home and Troy toward town. He had no Molly to call and he didn't want to go home to a father who would not be going fishing-hunting-bowling-boating-ball-playing with his son. It was as good a time as any, he decided, to see Mr. Hutton and find out what was going on for next week's paper. Who knows, he thought, he might even do the drawings over the weekend and not wait until the last minute as usual.

Early Saturday mornings the town was even emptier than on weekdays. The only action was at the hardware store. Princess Avenue stretched out before him, down past Grand Square, disappearing beneath the reaching arms of oak trees.

As he opened the door to the newspaper office the bells jangled. "It's me, Troy," he called out, and he crossed the small front office to the door of Mr. Hutton's office, first door off the hallway.

"Good morning, Troy," Mr. Hutton said from where he sat typing. "You're off to an early start for a Saturday."

"I'm always off to an early start," Troy said. "Especially on Saturdays. Saturdays and Sundays are *my* days and I don't like to waste a minute of them."

Mr. Hutton laughed. "Not so at my house," he said. "I left all my girls sleeping."

"Are we going to do anything about American Newspaper Week?" Troy asked.

"How did you know about that?"

"I keep up," Troy said. He'd never sprung his daily data trick on Mr. Hutton, but he knew this from his Chases' Calendar.

The man nodded and smiled. "Yes, as a matter of fact I am. I thought I'd like a panel cartoon of all the ways people recycle the newspaper after they've read it. Variations on the old fish-wrapper theme. Everything from clipping for scrapbooks to lining trashcans. What do you think?"

"Yeah," Troy said. "And house-training puppies."

Mr. Hutton laughed. "You're pretty sharp, Troy. I like that. And how about some political cartoons? We have some elections coming up. If you have time, I'd like for you to go back to the morgue and look up pictures of each of the candidates and work up some caricatures. I don't mean I need the caricatures today. Make copies of the photos and take them home. What do you think?"

"I don't even know who the candidates are or what they're running for," Troy said. Nor did he have the vaguest notion of what to draw for a political cartoon.

"I can tell you don't read the paper," Mr. Hutton said, handing Troy a list of the candidates and the offices for which they were running. "They've all been in it."

Troy tilted his head, embarrassed.

"It's all right, it's all right," the editor said. "I'm just teasing you. But be prepared to have some fun with this."

"What do you mean?" He was afraid Mr. Hutton was about to ask the impossible.

84

"You are about to begin your career as a political cartoonist," Mr. Hutton said. "I'll supply the captions and you do the drawings."

"Oh, oh, okay, sure," Troy said, nodding with relief. The drawing he could handle as long as Mr. Hutton came up with the ideas. "All right. I think this will be fun." Smiling to himself, he walked back to the morgue, where all the back issues of the newspaper were kept. And he walked straight into Liesl Trunzo.

"Oh," he said in surprise.

"O. Henry," she said back. She was sitting at a large table surrounded by newspapers. Her dark-rimmed blue eyes perked with teasing.

"No, actually, today it's Michael Faraday."

"On this date in . . . ?" she said.

"Seventeen-ninety-one," he filled in. "It's also the anniversary of Tacy Richardson's ride. On this date in 1777. You can take your choice."

"You're into early American history today, I see," she said.

"Well, no, actually. Faraday was English. An early experimenter with electricity. And Tacy Richardson was a young woman who, fearing naught, rode her horse Fearnaught through dangerous territory to warn General Washington of the approach of the British."

"Do you know everthing?" she asked. A skein of hair fell forward of her shoulder as she cocked her head.

"Almost," he said, hoping his eyes danced toward her as hers seemed to be dancing toward him. "It's also the day of the Pennsylvania Bedmaking Championships in Philadelphia."

She laughed and clapped her hands in delight and the lariat of her laughter tied his tongue for a moment. There was a green silence onto which he blurted, "What are you

85

doing here?" As he asked the question, he moved toward where she sat and looked at the papers spread out on the table.

"I'm looking for old dance pictures," she said. He saw various poses of girls in tights and tutus. Terrible photography, he noted. Her thumb shuffled across the edge of a stack of papers. "There are tons of them," she said.

"What do you need them for?"

"I'm working on the history of dance in Hanover."

For once he was glad to be tongue-tied in front of her because it kept back the sarcastic remarks that arose within him. The history of dance in Hanover? He didn't know whether that was deadly dull or highly hilarious. Or both. But, whatever, here was Liesl sitting before him like a gift. "Hey, look, a guy," he said, pointing to one photo. "A guy in ballet in Hanover, Georgia?" He leaned over to read the name, which he didn't recognize.

"Yes. One boy. Ten years ago," she said. "The boys in Hanover aren't macho enough to dance."

"Not macho enough!" he said. The words emerged more vociferously than he intended. "You mean too macho?" What kind of name was Trunzo? he wondered. She had sort of an Italian look about her. A thin face, dark hair, and thick dark lashes edging her deep blue eyes.

"No, I mean not macho enough. Like Russian men. Don't you know that the male dancers in Russia are the heroes of the country? It takes a real man to be a dancer."

Her words so totally flabbergasted him that he lost what equilibrium he had gained since walking in and finding her here. In his discomfort he idly and without thought did what he did best. He stepped backward to the doorway and swung one leg, toes aiming for the top of the door frame. Something about this astonished her. Her brows raised and her jaw dropped and her mouth

86

gaped as though staring like her eyes. Kick, kick, kick, he continued the motion, willing his muscles to direct the rest of himself into familiar patterns. She kept watching, kept staring until even his muscles fell out of synchronization.

"Why are you staring?" he asked, both feet on the floor again, one shoulder against the door frame so she couldn't see he'd turned flaccid.

"You're a dancer!"

"Karate," he said, letting a hand fly with a strike and following it with a sidekick.

"You're a dancer," she repeated.

To tease her, to please her, he duplicated what he remembered of her routine in front of the *Historian* window, pirouetting, sweeping his arms from above his head to his feet.

Pressing an index finger to her lips, she said, "Oh, Troy, would you, would you, would you?" With her finger holding them in place, her lips barely moved as they formed the words.

Would he, would he, would he what? he wondered. He was so captivated by her charming, imploring look, that marvelously delicate finger at the lips, that he would, he would, he would. Jump off the River Bridge? Fly to Philadelphia to enter the bedmaking championships? Spend days here in the morgue helping her find pictures of quondam Hanover dancers? He would do it, he would do it, even though he could barely form the words and push them from his mouth.

"Would I do what?" he managed to ask, knowing he would do whatever she asked. He murmured internal apologies to Darius, who even at this moment was probably talking to Molly. He had heard of love at first sight but never given it thought, never thought about love at all, and here it was bursting all around him, in him, from him. Here was Liesl asking if he would.

"Would you, would you, would you come to dance class? Oh, would you? We're doing *Coppélia* and I have the lead and Mrs. Thompson is going to do Franz only because we don't have any boys. Would you come and be my Franz? Please?" She had stood up and come around the table and taken his hand and dropped into a swooping curtsy.

Would he, would he, would he? Come to dance class? Ballet class? Time stretched out on wings of lost hope as his larynx struggled for the right words. There were no right words, no words at all to describe so swift a comedown.

"Me? In dance class?" he said finally, his voice tight, the words tight. "Not hardly," he said.

"My mistake," she said, reversing the elegant curtsy and returning to the chair at the table. "I thought you were man enough."

"You want Darius," he said. "Darius Callway." He didn't know what words he fumbled out or why. In the midst of them he as much as ridiculed Darius for the musical kata. In his mind he fled, left the situation behind. Love had begun and ended so swiftly. Obviously, Liesl was not going to be his Molly. But he stayed, somehow, pulling out old issues of the paper, using the copy machine to make copies of pictures of the local politicos.

"What are you doing?" she asked after a while.

He told her, finished making copies, returned the papers to the file. She was getting ready to go too. It would be so easy, he thought, to tell her it was the birthday of the ice-cream cone and invite her to come get one with him.

"If you change your mind," she said, "come to the

Hanover Dance Studio at the Rec Park Tuesday night at seven-thirty."

He turned to go out the door. "Tuesday is the beginning of American Newspaper week," he said. He walked down the hall without saying, "On this date in 1690 . . ."

9

*W*ith the newspaper photos of local political hopefuls in hand, Troy trudged home. Mother and Dad were in the living room reading. He almost opened his mouth and voiced his "Read, read, read" complaint, but instead he waved the newspaper clippings at them and told them what his next project was for the *Historian*.

"And speaking of projects, did I tell you that Roger Cheney asked me to be in charge of a karate demonstration for some muscular-dystrophy kids?" He told them about it and about the routines he and Keven and Darius had worked out.

"Mr. Cheney must really think a lot of you to give you that responsibility," Mother said.

Troy squirmed at the use of "Mister" when referring to Cheney. They didn't know, wouldn't care, or else would be glad to know that *Mr.* Cheney had postponed his black-belt test. This demonstration was like a test. Would Cheney have put him in charge otherwise? It wasn't the huge compliment Mother seemed to think. He shrugged.

"Sounds great," Dad said. "When is it?"

"Friday, October 5," Troy said. "Chester A. Arthur's birthday. It's also a teachers' workday." He looked at Mom. Instead of pleasing him, their perk of interest irritated him. He started toward the hall and paused to say, "I'm not at all sure that kids with muscular dystrophy will

90

appreciate seeing a karate demonstration. And I'm not at all sure I appreciate your interest."

"Whoa," Dad said. "Come back in here. It seems we have a couple of things to talk about." Troy stood where he was at the edge of the hall. "Come on back," Dad said. Troy came. "Sit down," Dad said. Troy remained standing and fixed his hands on the back of the sofa.

"Let's start with the easy one," Dad said. "Why do you think the kids with muscular dystrophy would not enjoy a karate demonstration?"

Troy sighed and slumped. "The answer is obvious," he said.

"Then I'm blind to the obvious," Dad said, "which I may be on many occasions."

Troy thought of telling them it was a national holiday in the Republic of Mali. On this date in 1960 . . .

Mother's voice brought his mind back to the subject. "Is it because they're handicapped and you think it might be hurtful for them to see this physical adroitness?"

Troy was still standing slumped at the back of the sofa. Although he didn't know the word "adroit" he fully understood what she meant. Nonetheless he said, "Adroitness? If you're going to talk to me, could you please use English?"

"I know you are bright enough to comprehend the word in the context in which I used it," she said. "Now, will you answer my question?"

"What question was that?" he said. All he wanted to do was stomp off to his room and be done with it.

"Troy," Mother said in a warning tone.

He sighed again. "Something like that," he said.

"If you're upset about this, why didn't you ask Mr. Cheney to assign it to someone else?"

Troy expelled air forcefully and fell forward onto the

sofa, flipping to a lengthwise position as he landed. For a while he just lay there.

"Well?" she said.

In a swift stream of words he said, "Because-I-was-disqualified-from-the-tournament-last-Saturday-and-he-postponed-my-black-belt-test-and-has-given-me-this-as-a-test-instead." He ended his words by folding his arms across his chest, clutching the pain which rose as fresh as last Saturday.

"Oh, Troy," Mother said, elongating both words.

"Troy, son, I'm sorry. What happened?"

He stared at the off-white ceiling and noticed a spot and wondered how it had gotten there. He knew it wasn't from his toe. These were ten-foot ceilings. He'd never kicked that high. How could he tell his mild-mannered parents what had happened? The spot on the ceiling activated, became a small screen, and he saw himself and Dwight mixing it up, losing control, being warned, being ousted, but the anger was on the ceiling and not within him.

"I lost my temper," he said finally.

"Oh, Troy," Mother said. He didn't move a muscle, but prepared for their lecture on "temper." "You must have felt terrible about it."

"We know how hard you've worked," Dad said.

Warmth flashed over him, then guilt, then both receded. Here they were being instantly sympathetic. Some parents, Keven's for instance, would pounce and denounce and demand to know what terrible thing he'd done to be disqualified. The moment was brief, not potent enough to overcome his distress and irritation. He sat up, and told them about being assigned the demonstration.

"So, you see," he said, "I have to do it."

"Well, no," Dad said. "Of course you don't. Make that clear in your mind. There are some things in life that you have to do, but this is not one of them. You want to do this, you choose to do this because it clears the path for something else that is important to you."

"Split hairs," Troy said.

"No," Dad said. "It is a fine point and many people never have the insight to grasp it, but it is not split. Some of life just happens, son, and we can't help it. But there are many definite choices that either clog or clear our paths. You have chosen to accept the assignment for this demonstration because it will clear the path for you to take the black-belt test. It is a good decision. But don't confuse it with something you *have* to do, as though there were no choice."

"Polydectes," Troy said.

"Now who's not speaking English?" Mother asked.

"He's speaking Greek mythology," Dad said.

"What gets me," Troy said, arms still folded across his chest, "is the way you two are suddenly interested in what I'm doing with karate, something you approve of, when it is something that doesn't mean anything to me and I have tried, tried . . ." The smell of damp, hot salt filled his head and his voice threatened to drown in it. Before his voice could quiver, he stopped talking and breathed deeply. But the air, instead of quelling his voice, created a draft and lifted it. Words rose out of him in another stream.

"I have tried, I have wanted, I have practically begged for you to be interested in karate. Just a little. Just because . . . just because I like it and I am your son." Fluid had collected at the corner of one eye and he broke his hold on himself to swipe at it viciously and he sprang to a sitting position.

"I mean, Nick and Keven are on a fishing trip together right now. Like a father and a son. They *do* some things together. Camping, fishing, hunting, all sorts of things." In lieu of having his arms across his chest to hold himself together, he clamped his teeth onto his lower lip. If all the rage came out, he would disintegrate.

Dad took in such a breath it almost created a vacuum in the room. "Troy. Oh, my, Troy. I am sorry." Dad's eyes closed for a moment. "Troy, I am so sorry. When is the next tournament?"

"The day after the demonstration for the muscular-dystrophy kids," Troy said. "In Savannah." As soon as he'd said it he was sorry. He clenched his teeth and spoke between them. "But if you think that coming to one tournament can make up for things—" He interrupted himself by charging up from the sofa and thudding down the hall to his room. There was only silence behind him. He could just see them looking at one another.

In his room he stood in the middle of it, in the space recluttered since his quick cleanup the other night. His breath came in drags and went in snorts. Finally he climbed the ladder and plunked down on his bed, pulling the curtain across to enclose himself. He stared into the blankness of the white ceiling four feet above him and bade his mind go blank.

Somewhere on the canvas of his mind he drew sketches of the future. He saw himself with his own son, first holding a small hand, then a larger one. He saw himself taking his boy swimming, camping, ball playing. His conscious mind intruded a bit and suggested that the child might be a girl. His pictures halted as he considered this and reconciled himself to a daughter. Sure. A father ought to do these things with a girl too. Maybe she'd even like karate. He reran the scenes, replacing the boy with a girl. The boy had been sturdy and blond. The girl was delicate, with dark hair, and he couldn't make her grow beyond the small, handholding size. With a start he realized she looked like Liesl. He rolled to his stomach and punched his pillow. His visions exploded and he thought: What if my son is like my father?

A knock sounded at the door, a slight, tentative knock. He didn't answer. The tap-tap-tap was repeated.

"Troy? Troy?" Dad's voice squeezed through the cracks of the door and floated to Troy's ears. "We need to talk, son. May I come in or would you prefer to come out?"

Neither, Troy thought. But when his parents decided to talk, he was in for a talk. That was not a choice. He curled his arms beneath the pillow and buried his chin in it. He wouldn't, couldn't move.

More knocks. "Troy?" his father asked.

"Come in," Troy said into the pillow.

Dad opened the door, came in, and closed it behind him.

Troy listened but could not tell where Dad stood in the room, or whether he sat. Dad didn't say anything. Troy wondered how long he would have to wait for this talk to begin, or was Dad waiting for him to pull back the curtain or poke his head out? He did neither. He clung to his position with the pillow. Instead of blank ceiling or mind he was staring into the mound of mess still on the other bed.

Cranes of Ibycus, he thought. That tangle of clothes and papers was ridiculous. Surely he could do something about that, at least.

"Troy, I am truly sorry," Dad began. Troy closed his eyes and prepared for the siege. "I have been blinded by my own distaste for fighting of any kind. The only time I could ever imagine fighting was when you were small. I would have protected you against anything, at any cost. But now you can take care of yourself in that regard better than I could take care of you."

Troy gave a muffled snort into the pillow.

"I have to admit that your mother and I both hoped you would outgrow your interest in karate, and this hope has kept us both from seeing how totally involved and absorbed you've become with this. I see now that you have a passion for it just as much as you do with your art, just as much as I do with photography and Mother with her music."

Troy made a different sort of huff into the pillow. Concession time, he thought.

"Just as we have to try to understand you, you have to try to understand us too. You haven't helped the situation with all your blood-and-guts talk, you know." Dad paused, as though he expected Troy to respond. Troy could not think of a single thing to say. What was there to say? He heard a slight ruffling sound like the flutter of wings or the shuffle of pages. Was it a bird, or wind from outside? Or was Dad going through some of his stuff? He almost moved to look, but he kept his resolve to be still.

"I'm coming to the next tournament," Dad said. "And Mother and I would like to come watch the demonstration if you don't think our presence would make you nervous."

This remark did make Troy bob his head a bit. Their presence make him nervous? At the moment he couldn't imagine that their presence would have any effect on him at all.

"I'll take some pictures, both at the demonstration and the tournament."

Troy opened his mouth and some rush of blood carried release to his brain cells. Pictures. Dad had never taken any pictures of him doing karate, not even him standing still in his gi. He saw shots in his head already, especially one of him in a midair flying sidekick.

"As for discussion number one, your feelings about the kids not wanting to see such a demonstration, your mother said that if something happened to her voice it wouldn't mean she'd never want to hear singing again."

In spite of himself Troy laughed.

"What's funny?" Dad asked.

"Darius," Troy said. "Darius said exactly the same thing."

"Well, it's apropos," Dad said.

There was another tentative knock on the door. "May I come in?" Mother asked. Troy laughed without sound this time. He could picture Mother standing outside the door, listening, trying to decide when or if her intrusion would be apropos.

"Troy?" Dad asked, to jog a response to Mother.

"Come in," Troy said.

"I've been looking at your Chases' Calendar here," Dad said, "and I see it's the birthday of the ice-cream cone."

Behind the curtain, Troy smiled at Dad's sleight-of-tongue. So that's what the rustling noise was, Dad looking at the Chases'.

"Why don't we all go get one?" Dad said.

"Good idea," Mother said.

"Count me out," Troy said. His mood had lightened but he still wasn't ready to be sociable.

"Aw, come on," Dad said. "We can celebrate Michael Faraday's birthday."

Troy smiled again, but still said, "Count me out, thanks."

"Well, listen to that, Mrs. Matthews," Dad said. "At

least he's polite about it. In spite of the ups and downs, I think the boy's had some good raising. Okay, Troy. Ice-cream cones are a choice, not a requirement. How about you, love?"

Troy didn't look but he imagined Dad scooping Mother around the waist and giving her a turn. The bedroom door closed, then another door, and he heard the car start. In another minute he sat up and slid to the floor without use of ladder. He started looking at the politico pictures and, soon after, began to sketch.

10

Monday was Schwenkenfelder Thanksgiving in the Pennsylvania Dutch country. Troy did not feel thankful. He was achingly aware that Keven and Nick were taking the black-belt test tonight. And unless there was some unusual circumstance, they would be awarded their belts. They'd be wearing flashy red gis to show off the belts.

In Carson City, Nevada, it was National Whistle-off Day, but Troy wasn't whistling, either. For some reason the ragoos laid off the hassle and Troy was glad. He was in a snarly enough mood to chew them up and spit them out and he knew they'd taste terrible. Besides, he had been thinking about what Dad said about choices. He needed to clear obstacles from his path toward his own black belt, not create them. And the ragoos certainly could be an obstacle.

Clearing the path was the only reason he went to karate class. He wanted to stay away, to plead virus, flu, or black plague. Even if he was truly stricken with some fatal disease, his absence would be taken as an excuse, and even, perhaps, as disrespect and lack of humility. So he went and watched Keven and Nick take the black-belt test without him. Had Nick ever asked about Keven's part in the sign business? If not, Troy knew why not. For this. For this exquisite father-son togetherness. Neither

Nick nor Keven would have spoiled this for the sake of truth. With bittersweetness he watched them execute everything perfectly, as he knew he could do himself. Even more painful was joining them afterward for the celebratory pizza. No one commented on his mood.

On Tuesday evening, to avoid any call to practice from Keven-the-black-belt, Troy set out for an idle walk. For no reason he walked away from the river, down the tree-sheltered streets. Mid-block every block he practiced a few techniques. He walked briskly but did not jog. Martial artists didn't jog. The rhythmic jouncing of jogging compressed the spongy disks of the spine until one actually lost some of the flexibility, the bend and twist of the backbone. Darius' father was a slender, in-good-shape jogger but he could not bend over and touch his toes.

Troy wondered if Liesl knew that today was the anniversary of Balboa's discovery of the Pacific Ocean. Pompous Balboa, he thought, to think the Indians didn't know the ocean was there. Or perhaps it was the history books that were pompous, and not Balboa at all. He had wanted to tell Liesl about Balboa, but there she was with Donnie Duggan again at school. What chance did he have against a junior? A Big Man on campus.

Low in the sky behind him the sun cast long shadows east. With the trees touching limbs across the street, the sunglow spilled down the street as though through a tunnel. Troy reverse-punched the late leaning shadows of trees, then executed a series of sidekicks, sliding his support foot as he turned and kicked to the points of the compass. On the other hand, he thought, what chance did Donnie Duggan have against him, Troy Matthews, artist and martial artist?

He found himself at Sidney Lanier Boulevard, across from the Rec Park, and he wandered across the street and beneath the entrance arch. To left and right were tennis

100

courts and ball fields, all full of the action of bounding balls. As he walked by the court the field lights came on, the rays diminished by the remaining daylight. As he entered the main Rec Park building the bleepity-bleepity-bleep of video games peppered his eardrums.

To give himself a reason for being here, he walked over to the Astro Fighters game, which was in use at the moment. He was not ready to admit his real reason, not ready to think of a dance class going on here somewhere.

"Winner," he said to the two combatants as he set a quarter on the side of the machine. The two players finished the game and the loser immediately set down a quarter to play the next winner. Troy made it straight through to refueling and all the way back to the greenies before taking a hit. By the third refueling he was losing patience with standing here. This was not calming his adrenaline but revving it. He was relieved when the other player took a third strike and lost the game. Without even finishing out his turn, he said, "You've got the loser this time."

"Really?" both boys said.

Those two could use a little karate confidence, he thought as he walked away. Another time he might even try to recruit them for class, but he needed all his energy for his own confidence at the moment.

He eyed the door to the auditorium and walked over to it. The intention was to pull the door open and quickly slip into a back seat and watch the proceedings for a few minutes. He had not come to dance, that was for sure. He'd come to watch because Liesl had asked him to come. He had to command himself to take hold of the door handle and pull. Then with no urging at all his feet skittered through the doorway and into the dark. Quickly. Zip. The door sighed to a close behind him.

It took a moment to realize the dark was total. There

101

were no lights even on the stage. There was no dance class in progress here. Leaning against the door and stepping backward, he opened it again. Light from the lobby filtered into the cavernous space.

"May I help you?" asked a young woman in a red-and-white Rec Park Staff T-shirt.

"Yeah, uh, well, I guess I have the wrong night," he said.

Liesl had said Tuesday, he was sure of it. Was this her idea of a joke, a way to get back at him for the way he'd acted when she'd invited him to come to class?

"What was it you came for?" the woman asked.

"Uh, nothing, well, uh, dance class. I was invited to come watch dance class."

"Oh, they're in the studio."

"The studio? Where's that? I thought they practiced in here." He was relieved to manage the words without another "uh."

She pointed across all the bleeping games. "Through that doorway, then it's the only door on the right."

Through that doorway? He turned to confirm the directions but she had walked away. The only thing he knew of that was through that doorway was the girls' rest room. The boys' rest room was on this side. He'd never been through that other doorway. That was . . . well, the girls' side. Through that doorway, she had said. Perhaps he'd just play another game or two and go on home. He glanced around to see which one he'd play, but he was reluctant to feed quarters to a machine. Four quarters made a dollar and dollars translated into karate lessons, equipment, and tournaments.

He realized he was staring across the bleeps at the door the woman had indicated. "Well, do it or don't do it, Matthews," he said to himself. Before he could think again he walked across the lobby and pushed open the intimidating door. He stood in a well-lighted hallway and whatever assault he expected did not occur. There was a pair of doors on the left and a single door on the right. The first door on the left was marked "Girls." The single door led to the dance studio. The word "studio" conjured a picture of the karate studio, which had a row of chairs against the wall nearest the door. A person could slip in, sit down, and watch without interrupting anything. Before he could lose his momentum, he pushed open the door on the right.

One step and he was in the midst of a hubbub of girls in leotards and tights. Bright lights and ballerinas bounded in reality and in reflection in the mirrored room. It was as though he had stepped into a girls' dressing room and no girl was dressed. Or perhaps it was he himself who was undressed. As quickly as he could, which was all too slowly, he reached behind him for the doorknob. Somehow it seemed important not to turn his back on them.

"Are you Troy?" a slender, girlish-looking woman asked.

"Uhhhh," he said.

"Liesl," the woman called. "Troy is here."

"Uhhh," he said again. He turned around, found the doorknob, clutched it, pulled it, and got himself back on the other side of it. It clicked closed behind him and he leaned against it. Almost immediately, it opened and he nearly fell backward into Liesl, who was coming through.

"Troy," she said. "Come on back in."

He jerked himself away from her, away from the door. "No," he said. There was no way he would reenter that starkly glaring room.

Liesl moved in front of him and took one of his hands in both of hers. "But you came," she said. "I knew you would."

She knew he would come? How could she possibly have known he would come? He hadn't known it himself until he got here, until he walked under the arches, until he opened the door of the electronic lobby. Finally, finally his throat recovered from paralysis and he spoke with a deadly calm. "How did you know I would come?"

She caught her lush pink bottom lip with her teeth. She still held on to his hand. There were only his hand and her hands between himself and her. There was a breeze from somewhere and he was flying like a kite, right here in the hallway, doing loop-the-loops along the ceiling, tethered only by her two hands holding his one hand. "Come on in," she said. "We need to practice."

Practice? Practice? She was really jumping to conclusions. He seemed to look down on her, not from just his taller height but from where he was fluttering against the ceiling. "Hasn't it occurred to you that I only came to watch?"

"No," she said. "I thought you came to dance with me."

Had she really said it? Dance with me? Had she said *dance with me*? Oh, oh, oh, how he wanted to dance with her. He saw the two of them on Princess Avenue dancing to the reflections of the street as though the street was the river and they were dancing on water.

"No," he said. "No." He would not, could not reenter that room with the leotarded girls multiplied in mirrors.

The door opened again. It was the girl-woman. "Are you coming, Liesl? Are you going to join us, Troy? We'd certainly like to have you."

"Mrs. Thompson, I think Troy is a little shy about it

right now," Liesl said. "Could we practice in the auditorium until he gets used to the idea?"

"Why, yes, Liesl, of course. What a thoughtful idea. Start teaching him the basics and I'll be along to help in a minute." The woman reentered the room and was swallowed by the closing door.

"We can go through the studio or through the lobby," Liesl said.

With a stuttering index finger Troy stabbed air in the direction of the lobby. He meant *out,* not to the auditorium. He wasn't going anywhere. He wasn't practicing anything. Where was his glib tongue? How could it have abandoned him at his moment of need?

"Okay," she said, stepping lightly ahead of him without relinquishing his hand. He tugged his hand free and reached over her to open the door. She no longer held his hand, but he still followed her as though connected. At the auditorium she opened the door, then transferred it to him. "Hold it a minute while I find the lights." He had barely taken hold of the door when blue-white strips of fluorescent lights rippled from above. When he stepped into the auditorium the door fell closed behind him with a whoomph of displaced air.

"There are five foot positions," she said, beginning to demonstrate, right there in the aisle. Her arms arced gracefully outward from shoulder to fingertips as though the bones themselves were fluid. In slow motion she placed her heels together with her toes pointing in opposite directions along a parallel line.

"This is first position," she said, and she stooped and rose, sweeping her arm down, across, and up as she moved. Keeping her feet parallel on the same line, she parted them a bit. "Second," she said, and she repeated the stooping, arm-sweeping motion. Then again, with

105

feet parallel on different lines, heel of right foot at the arch of the left, she stooped and swooped. "Third," she said. After she'd showed him the remaining two she began again with the first. "Come on," she said. "You do them."

His quick karate feet were immovable, leaden against the wood floor, the very sort of floor to which they were most accustomed.

"Come on," she said, repeating the positions in both word and action, flowing from one to the other.

Toward the end of the third sequence he began to mock her by duplicating her gestures in an exaggerated way. Feet nestled heel to toe, he stooped and rose and brandished his arm through the air. He assumed first position and dropped his body into the swoop. Down, up. Down, up. As he imitated her transitions the mockery vanished. Down, up. Down, up. Down, up.

To him she was the goddess Terpsichore, Muse of Dance. She needed no river mist to enchant her, no illusion of imagination. Here she was, real before him. He became her mirror image, a yard and a half distant, legs flowing, arms flowing, in reflection of hers. Mesmerized, he matched her motions, floating in place on the hard wood floor.

11

"Where were you last night?" Keven said, hailing Troy as he approached the school. "I thought we were going to practice."

Troy didn't think he could tell Darius, much less Keven, where he was last night. "I wandered down to the Rec and fed a few quarters to Astro Fighters," he said. A partial truth, he decided, was better than either the whole truth or a total lie.

"You?" Keven said, falling in beside Troy as they walked toward the building where they both had homerooms. "You're the one who says a video game is a waste of a good quarter. Well, we've got to get this demonstration down. It's just a week and two days away."

"The demonstration's down," Troy said. Keven's words rankled. Was Keven being overdiligent about the demonstration in apology for not having owned up to his part in the sign change for the ragoos? Or for having thus gotten out of the painting job? Or did Keven think he should have been asked to be in charge of the demonstration since he was the one who now had a black belt? Troy resented the intrusion of these thoughts because they nudged Liesl out of his head space, though he still saw her arms floating.

As soon as Troy and Keven moved onto the stairway

there was an exterior intrusion. Dwight and his cohorts were coming down the stairs.

"Oh, it's you," Troy said as the three closed the space on the stairway.

"Candleass, candleass, we'll get you," the boys said in unison. In a flowing movement the three parted, re-opened the space, and continued their downward journey. Keven laughed. Troy wondered if they'd been to ballet class.

After school he was surprised to hear Keven's question repeated by Dad. "Where were you last night?"

Dad had been in the darkroom when he'd come home and gone straight to his room. Awake or asleep, he had dreamed and danced all night.

"Why is everyone so interested in where I was last night?" he said. The words just popped out from glib brain to glib tongue. He was immediately sorry for his defensiveness, which would only cause more interest in where he was last night. Keven and Dad hardly constituted "everyone."

"Hey, it was just a question, not an inquisition," Dad said. "Sit down."

Uh-oh, Troy thought. Now it becomes an inquisition. Should he kneel as was done in medieval times, or simply sit? He sat. His head was already trying to think of diversions. He would have to play wounded grouse to draw Dad away from the real trail.

"I'm not prying, just interested," Dad said. "Your mother said you were home a little after nine. You're certainly old enough for that."

So it was Dad-ready-to-be-folksy-friends time, Troy thought. It happened periodically and, Troy thought, after what happened between them on Saturday there would be a campaign. He heard Mother's car pull into the carport, heard the car door slam and the kitchen door open. She did not call out either to him or to Dad. Uh-oh, he thought. That meant she knew there was "a talk" going on. He wondered if the talk was supposed to be about last night or about last Saturday.

"You know, we try to give you your head, give you independence. We've tried very hard not to be possessive, as many parents of only children are."

Troy nodded. That was true. Dad was making the effort. Dad was at least making an effort. Troy thought he should be making a corresponding effort.

"I was just out walking," he said.

Dad nodded. "I know how you like to walk."

The exchange was inadequate, Troy knew. He felt the spareness of it, and scrabbled around inside himself for something to fill the space between the two of them sitting here at right angles in the living room. Liesl kept turning in his head, filling him to bursting. He wanted to be the very best Troy Matthews for her and for himself. And for Dad too? Maybe he'd let just a little bit of Liesl slide into the conversation.

"Well," he said when the pause seemed interminable. "There's this girl." He realized his timing was all wrong. The long pause increased the importance of what he said.

"Ah," Dad said. "I wondered if that might be the case. Might I know her name?"

The way Dad worded himself was sometimes archaic, Troy thought. But he had no reluctance about answering. He wanted to say her name: Liesl, Liesl, Liesl. So he said it.

"Liesl."

"Oh, Liesl Trunzo," Dad said.

Troy was startled. Now Dad knew more than he intended. "How did you know that?" he asked, closing himself off again, sorry he'd ever opened.

"Oh, come on, Troy. How many Liesls are there running around?"

Troy nodded and gave half a grin. "Right," he said. There were no other Liesls running around.

"Besides, I've known Liesl's mother since high school. We went to Hanover Academy together back in the Dark Ages. She lived away for a number of years but moved back a year or so ago and married Bill Duggan. You know Mr. Duggan."

"Who?" Troy said, though he'd heard perfectly well. He just didn't believe what he'd heard. The name Duggan was rebounding in his head.

"Bill Duggan. You know. The school psychologist. I took you over there to look through his telescope when you were little. He's an excellent amateur astronomer."

The last of Dad's sentence was lost in Troy's whoop. He leapt up with a thrust fist leading him into the air. "That's it," he shouted. "He's her brother. Her stepbrother." All this time he hadn't known. He kept seeing her with him and hadn't known. "He's her brother. He's her brother!" He burst into a spray of karate techniques, punching and kicking air all over the room. Donnie Duggan was not a rival but a brother. "I thought . . ." he said, not finishing.

Dad grinned, "I know what you thought. So that's where you were last night."

Troy had sat back down and Dad's words nearly bounced him up again. "Uh, well, no, uh," he said, fumbling. He could tell Dad where he wasn't but not where he was. How had he managed to get himself caught in this trap? "I was just walking around thinking about her," he said. And when he said it he knew it was the truth. As he karate-chopped his way down the shadowy streets, subconscious thoughts of her had led him straight to the Rec Center. And she had known he would come when he hadn't known it himself.

"You and she are not sneaking around to see each other, are you?" Dad asked.

"Of course not," Troy exploded, anger propelling him to his feet again. He was bounding up and down like a pogo stick. "If I was doing that, I wouldn't have said anything to you about it, would I?" How had this turned awkward again? His anger was in knowing how close Dad was to knowing.

Mother walked in as defuser, eyebrows curved in question as though she hadn't been standing down the hall listening to every word. "What's going on?" she asked.

Troy looked at her and shook his head. He wasn't going to tell her what was going on when she already knew.

"I haven't hugged my boy today," she said, coming over and giving him a full, squeezing hug.

"Uh, look," he said when she'd released him. "I'm not doing anything wrong, all right? I wouldn't sneak around, and everything's okay. And there's something I have to do in town." He was gesturing this way and that and he felt like an idiot, but he had to get out of this somehow. All the thoughts about being the best Troy Matthews for Liesl made him think of the glass broken at the tip of Clark Gable's nose and how the best Troy Matthews would have fixed it by now.

"Something at the *Historian*?" Mother asked.

Well, close enough, he thought. "Yeah," he said. "And today's Johnny Appleseed's birthday. Do we have any apples?" He veered past Mother, through dining room to kitchen, and found three apples in the wooden fruit bowl. He picked up all three and juggled his way back to the living room. "Here, catch," he called, tossing one apple to Dad and one to Mother. As they each caught an apple, he caught the doorknob and went out.

He seemed to recall that there was an "In case of emergency call So-and-so" sticker on the door of the old theater. He would get the number and call it from the *Historian* office and that would make his answer true. Instead of crossing to the river he walked straight up Duke Street to town. He found the sticker he had envisioned but he had nothing to write it down with. Repeating the number to himself for memory, he walked the half-block to the newspaper office. He found a rhythm to the number and by the time he jangled the bells on the newspaper-office doorknob he was really stepping.

"Sure," Mr. Hutton said when Troy asked to use the phone. "Think you'll be ready to try a political sketch for next week?"

Troy nodded, said the number aloud, and reached for Mr. Hutton's pencil and notepad to write it down. "Excuse me," he said. "I'm about to forget the number." He launched into telling Mr. Hutton what had happened, though he neglected to say it happened a week ago.

"Well, I think the macho opportunist Rhett Butler deserves a kick in the keezer," Mr. Hutton said.

Troy used a phone in another room, reached the owner of the Ritz, and explained.

"Well, I certainly appreciate your honesty in owning up to it," the man said. "But with everything that needs to be done to the building, a broken display glass is a small matter. So, thanks for calling, but you can just forget it."

Troy hung up the phone in distress. The man had said

forget it. Why didn't that delight him? The man had granted him the gift of a clear conscience and saved him time and money as well. He went back to Mr. Hutton's office and told him what happened.

"Every time I pass the theater, that toe hole will glare at me like an evil eye. I won't feel right about it," Troy said.

"Let me call him," Mr. Hutton said. He dialed the number and his side of the conversation about young people and responsibility was sensible and gracious. Troy wondered if he would ever be able to handle his words so skillfully.

Mr. Hutton set the phone back on the cradle. "Do you know how to replace glass?"

Troy shook his head. "I guess I'm about to learn."

"Atlantic Glass is right there on River Street," Mr. Hutton said. "They'll cut a piece to size and probably give you the short course. Do you have anything to measure with?" Even before Troy shook his head again, Mr. Hutton was handing him a yardstick, then pencil and paper for writing down the measurements.

As he walked back to the Ritz, Troy was smiling. He liked Mr. Hutton's assumption that if he wanted or needed help he would ask for it. He unfastened the glass case and checked the measurements several times and studied the way the glass was put in. There was a strip of crumbling putty or caulking holding the glass.

"It's a rather tricky procedure," the man at the glass company said. "We'll be glad to do it for you."

"Yes," Troy said, "and charge me the price, too, I'll bet."

The man shrugged and acknowledged that he would have to charge something for the labor, of course. "But I'll give you a deal."

Troy didn't want a deal. Somehow, for Liesl, for Cheney, for himself, it was important to actually do the work himself, just like he'd fixed the dimmer switch and painted the door. Forgetting it, as the theater owner had suggested, was too easy. Having it done for him, even if he had been willing and able to pay for it, was also too easy. The man gave him the short course on replacing glass and sold him caulk and a caulk gun in addition to the glass. The price of these things set him back a new gi.

As he moved his finger along the caulk line to seal it to glass and frame, he thought: I know how to replace a broken pane of glass. It wasn't all that tricky an operation. It just involved some of those tiny necessary bits of knowledge that make things easier. He examined his work with pleasure and saw a blob of caulk inside the frame where it was too thick.

Well, too late now, he thought. In order to remove the blob the glass would have to be taken out, and he wasn't going to do that. Still, it was a good job. He closed the frame and pressed it until he heard the notches click. Still, he double-checked and triple-checked to be sure the frame was firmly closed. If the thing fell open when he let go, and the glass fell out, he'd fall out too, he thought. Slowly he removed his hands from the side of the frame, keeping his hands a few inches away as though still holding it. Nothing moved. He winked at Clark Gable.

Finally, when he was sure nothing would go amiss, he let his hands drop. He gazed at his work as though it was art. Well, it was, he thought. There was every bit as much effort and know-how in replacing a pane of glass as in drawing a cartoon. He smiled and bobbed his head with pleasure. Before his head had stopped moving from the bob, something whizzed past his ear.

There was a crash and glass started falling from the frame.

114

12

*T*he rock might as well have been a boulder and struck Troy in the head. As quickly as the golf-ball-size stone lodged against Scarlett O'Hara's collarbone, he snapped his head around. Curly-haired Stuart was fleeing behind tall Dwight, and it was undoubtedly Bert's sneakered feet disappearing around the corner. Troy turned back, leaned forward, and replaced his hands on the frame of the display case as though this would reverse what had just happened. He didn't know whether he wanted to cry or kill. Shards of glass sprinkled the toes of his sneakers, and incredibly, the original glass with its tiny hole and flaring spiderweb cracks still stood intact. He stood up straight and swallowed. His breath trembled as it went in and out. Suddenly he whirled, as if he could now catch them and dash their brains out against the nearest building. The raging adrenaline urged him to pop off in all directions, and he ran around the corner after them, then back to Grand Square, as though this was the central point for a search. He started north, east, south, west, then ran west, back past the Ritz without even glancing at the Clark Gable lobby card or the broken glass in the alcove. Nor did he notice the *Historian* office or the hardware store as he ran by.

At the river he slowed his pace to a brisk walk, willing the Altamaha-ha to rise, willing her to skim along the surface of the water and give him solace. But she did not appear. He punched toward the ground as though this action would pop her to the surface, but she did not come. He broke into a run. Keven was right. The Ha-ha was of no use. He was foolish to try to salve himself with a creature of his own imagination.

A pain pierced his side. He gave in to it for a moment only, and continued to run. He hadn't had a stitch in his side since he was eight or nine; he had too much stamina and body control for that. Emotional pain centered in the side, his anger at the dragoons, his sadness at finding no rescue at the river. He darted east on Oglethorpe toward Duke, toward home, knowing that home would not provide consolation either. He bounded in the front door and ran to his room, opening and closing the door even faster than he had the door to the ballet studio last night. Putting one foot onto a middle rung of the ladder, he flung himself onto the bunk.

"Troy, is that you?" came his mother's voice.

Now, who else did she think it could be? he wondered.

"Are you all right?" Dad opened the door, something neither of his parents ever did without knocking and receiving permission.

"Leave me alone," Troy said.

"Something wrong at the paper?" Dad asked.

"No," Troy said sharply.

Dad nodded. "Well, whatever it is, I'm sorry. We're both sorry." Dad retreated and reclosed the door. Troy knew they thought the problem was with Liesl. Well, good. Let them draw their own conclusions.

Hands clenched at his sides, he plotted every possible and impossible confrontation with the dragoons. He didn't care which one of them actually threw the rock, he considered them equally guilty. He would not be satis-

116

fied until he smashed all three. The black belt was no longer important enough to restrain him, nor was the possibility of getting in trouble at school. In most of his imaginings he was the easy victor. But even if they managed to mangle him, he would not stop as long as he had at least one movable muscle.

As he approached school Thursday morning he was six-eyed, and all eyes were looking for dragoons. In the hall, on the stairs, everywhere, he looked for them. Whereas dragoons had been popping out at him from everywhere, now he couldn't find one. Psychic vibes of his homicidal intent must be giving out warning rays, he thought. But that was all right. He'd get them. They had followed him and hounded him, as pesky as gnats, until they learned his schedule. He could do the same with them. He would get them.

As he moved between classes his eyes moved independently, like chameleon eyes, like Dad's eyes when he was giving half-attention.

"What's with you today," Keven asked.

"This is the day," Troy said. "This is the day when I dragoon the ragoos. Devastate, demolish, destroy."

"Wha-a?" Keven asked.

"Enough of aggravation. Enough of pestation. I'm going to pulverize them, crunch them into gravel, and use them to pave my driveway." He was concentrating so on the search for dragoons that he was quite taken aback to hear Liesl's voice.

"What day is it today?" she asked.

"This is National Dried Fig Week," he said. The calendar information came out automatically. How had she come up on him so suddenly when he had been watching so carefully?

"I wondered if we could get together sometime.

Maybe Saturday," she said. "I could tell you the story of *Coppélia* and let you listen to the music. It's wonderful music. I know you'll like it."

He was looking over her shoulder, scanning the between-periods hallway for any sign of dragoons. "Uh," he said in response to her question. Saturday was only two days away but he couldn't see Saturday from here. "I don't know, uh, I don't know what I've got for Saturday."

"Well, I just thought . . ." she said, letting her voice trail off at the peal of the bell. "Well, I've got to go," she said, and they darted to their respective classrooms.

At his desk he realized he'd just done something stupid. But could he help it if he was distracted? If getting the dragoons was more important than his black belt, it was also more important than . . . He caught himself at the thought. Yeah, go on and tell yourself that, he chided himself. Getting the dragoons is more important than getting Liesl? He pounded the desk with his fist. The teacher looked at him and he gave an apologetic look. He remembered an experiment Miss Clutz had given them, telling them to spend sixty seconds looking around the room for things that were red. When the time was up, she asked them to name all the green things in the room. They protested that she had said red. "Don't ever narrow your focus so that you don't see everything around you," she'd told them. And he'd just narrowed Liesl right out of his focus.

Between the last two periods he spotted Dwight, that head above all the other heads, at the other end of the hall. Set for action, he didn't waste a moment before he sprinted and bob-shouldered his way through the stream of students. He willed Dwight to remain in the hall and not disappear into one of the rooms. Dwight's back was

118

to him. He reached up and out and spun the boy around, ready with a front thrust.

Someone grabbed his arm and stepped inside his range. It was Keven, saying, "No, man, no. Don't do this, man."

Dwight used the moment to step back. Troy jerked away from Keven and kicked out at Dwight. Keven grabbed Troy again, spoiling his kick. "You don't know anything about this," Troy said to Keven. He couldn't believe this was Keven holding him back. "Come on, Kev, this is our chance." Keven had been itching for a fight. They could have their test of strength and skill right now, Troy thought. Troy and Dwight. Or Troy and Keven if that's what Keven preferred.

What stopped him was not Keven's hold but the rerun of his own words. "You don't know anything about this." The words sank in like a slow-motion kick to the groin. Keven didn't know anything about this. Darius didn't know anything about this. Nick, Cheney, Mom, Dad, no one knew anything about this. Why, he wondered, why? Only Harvey Hutton and the theater owner knew about the initial broken window. Only he and the ragoos knew about the subsequent one. He had shared so much with Keven and Darius. He had shared his life with them. Why had he not told them about the twice-broken window? What was going on with him? The bell rang again and he was a long hallway away from class. The day had gone by in these between-class segments. And now it was time for history. What he didn't want to do right now was sit in history class listening to the teacher drone on about long-dead people as though they had never been alive. What he wanted to do was kill a dragoon and go home.

"You okay, man?" Keven asked. Dwight and the rest

of the student body had disappeared as though they all wore Pluto's helmet.

Troy shook his head. No, he wasn't all right. He wouldn't be all right until he had visited just punishment on the heads of Dwight, Bert, and Stuart. He and Keven walked down the hall and, with a concerned look, Keven slipped into his classroom. Troy passed the door to his history class and when he saw he'd done it, he quickened his pace. At the end of the hall he pounded down the stairs, out of the building, across campus, to his homeroom building. The door to the art room was open and there were only a few students inside beginning to work. Just as he was about to put his body into reverse, Miss Clutz looked up.

"Troy?" she said. "Come in. It's quite all right. This is the independent-study group."

He didn't know what the independent-study group was, but the smell of clay and paint filled him as surely as the smell of sweaty bodies. Here was solace.

"What can I do for you, Troy?" Miss Clutz asked.

Troy bobbed slightly from side to side. Here was where he wanted to be. "Can I stay in here this period?" he asked.

Miss Clutz studied him for a moment. "Are you in trouble about something?"

"No. No, ma'am, nothing like that. I just . . ." He shrugged his shoulders. He just what? What could he tell her? He needed a cocoon and this was it?

"Ah," she said. "Are you troubled about something?"

He started to deny it, but why else was he here instead of in history class? "Sort of," he said.

"Where are you supposed to be this period?" she asked.

"History," he said, dropping his head. He had already

120

been stupid about Liesl and now he was being stupid about Miss Clutz. No matter how much he liked her, Miss Clutz was a teacher. He shook his lowered head and wondered at his own stupidity.

"Here," she said, handing him a piece of paper.

"What's this?" He hadn't seen her write the note. A late slip, he thought.

"I've asked your history teacher to borrow you for this period," she said. "Go take it and have it signed. If you don't return, I'll know permission was not granted." If Miss Clutz were younger—even twenty-five wouldn't be too old—he would be in love with her instead of Liesl, he thought. Miss Clutz winked at him. "We won't make a habit of this," she said.

Now that he was there, he didn't know what he wanted to do with this extra time in the art room. He sat at one of the tables with pencil in hand and paper under hand. As he looked about the room at the other students bent in concentration over their work, he began sketching them. Good, he thought. This was a chance to practice likenesses in preparation for the caricatures Mr. Hutton wanted. His hand moved quickly, making marks on paper, the work coming from some deeply interior source.

A nearby gasp brought him out of his creative reverie. "She'll have a fit," said one of the nearby students who was looking at his work. Only then did he realize he had sketched a likeness of Miss Clutz. He was startled, pierced by the student's comment. However subconsciously he'd made the drawing, it had been done with love. Would Miss Clutz have a fit? Would she think he was making fun of her? Before he could think to shield it, there was Miss Clutz behind him, making rounds.

"Troy, these are wonderful," she said, seeing the

121

sketches of the students. He held his breath as her eyes fell on the caricature of herself, with exaggerated bun, beak, and bifocals. She picked it up and held it out for a better perspective.

"Oh, Troy," she said. "I love it! May I have it? May I please have it?"

13

*A*fter school Troy tramped home and holed up in his room and worked on the caricatures for the paper. The extra time in the art room had not quelled his murderous intent but he hadn't even seen another dragoon after Dwight.

One of the political candidates had a high forehead, so Troy exaggerated it. Another had a large nose and small eyes which he featured prominently. A woman aspirant had a carefully elaborate hairstyle which he stressed. Once the pencil was moving the exterior world retreated. This was his cocoon. He was inside a bubble, the radius of which was not beyond his fingertips.

The pencil moved easily from political candidates to dancers. First position, second position, third position, fourth. Though inanimate, only number-two-lead markings on paper, the dancers moved and swayed. He suddenly realized what he was doing and laughed at himself for so pleasantly straying from the intended work. The dancers, he noted, had Liesl's face, Liesl's body. He smacked his fist down on the desk and broke his reverie. How could he have been so stupid when he saw her today? She had come up to him talking and making suggestions that they get together and he had practically ignored her. Did he really have his priorities that skewed?

Well, he'd call her, he thought. He looked toward the

123

door, trying to convince himself how easy it would be to go to the phone and call her. At least he knew to look up Duggan instead of Trunzo. He could apologize for being preoccupied and say he would like to see her on Saturday. Or he didn't have to say anything about being preoccupied. He could just say that he would like to acknowledge and say yes to her suggestion.

He was furious with the dragoons for more than broken glass now. What he should do, he thought, was look in the phone book for their addresses. What he should do was go to their houses and paint their doors and break their windows. And their necks. He began sketching dragoons. Long, lanky Dwight was the easiest to convey to paper. Stuart's curly hair was easy but he couldn't get the face right. Stuart had such a conventional face. He'd like to hold a convention all over Stuart's face. He began drawing what he drew more often than anything else, small figures sparring across the page. He drew himself into the pictures and kicked the tall one up into a live-oak tree and left him draping over a limb. He wrapped Bert around a fire hydrant and dismembered Stuart so totally that Stuart's body parts oozed through the holes of a sewer cover, dripping Stuart to where all three dragoons belonged. And Troy's own hair and gi were not even mussed.

Transferring the pencil from fingers to fist, he stabbed the paper repeatedly, pounding holes through Dwight, Bert, and Stuart as well as through several pages of his art pad.

"Hey, what's going on in there?" Dad called.

In karate class that night he was off balance from the start. He couldn't concentrate on meditation, couldn't stretch out properly. His muscles were tight and hard.

"Troy, what's with you tonight?" Cheney asked.

What's with this "what's with" business? Troy thought. What was with anybody? What was with someone throwing a rock and smashing glass?

"Are you sore?" Cheney asked.

Troy almost laughed. Sore did not come close to describing what he was! But Cheney meant physically. "Nah," he said, extending a slow-motion sidekick to prove his stability and control.

At break Cheney called to him and nodded toward the office. Troy raised his eyebrows and followed.

"What's going on, Troy? You're not yourself tonight."

"I'm a little off, that's all," Troy said smoothly.

"It's not like you to be a little off," Cheney said. "Have you slacked up on your workouts?"

"No!" Troy said. How could Cheney even think that?

"Is there a particular problem? Are you upset with me because I didn't let you take your black-belt test?"

"No, sir, no. It's not that. I understand about that." He grinned. "I'm embracing it." Just the same, he felt a sense of loss somewhere inside. Cheney was so far off target, yet Troy did not want to say anything to make the target more clear. There was no use talking to anyone about this. Dad, Miss Clutz, Cheney, Darius, would all manage to minimize the incident and try to talk him out of his murderous thoughts. Even Keven, *Keven,* had stopped him at school today.

Cheney sat at the desk idly rolling a pencil back and forth beneath his open hand. "Are you having any difficulty with the demonstration? It's next Friday, you know."

"Oh, yes, sir. No, sir," Troy said, responding in reverse.

"Well, look, you know you can talk to me anytime about anything," Cheney said.

Troy nodded.

"I'm not worried about you, Troy," Cheney said as he stood up. "You're made of good, solid stuff, inside and out."

After second-half meditation, just before the sparring, Cheney said to all of them, "Remember, you will never win if you have to prove yourself the winner."

Troy thought the remark was pointed directly at him, as though Cheney knew what was going on in spite of Troy not having told him. As he worked on techniques with a twelve-year-old blue belt, he worked over Cheney's words. You had to win to prove yourself the winner, so what did Cheney mean? The only way to come out on top was to come out on top.

He danced and dodged around the little kid who was trying to score on the big brown belt. The boy was good and had been progressing steadily. Still, Troy parried him easily.

"Good jab," he said to give encouragement. "You almost nailed me there." Troy was downplaying his own expertise so the boy could practice. "Don't be afraid to step in close," he said. To demonstrate, he kept budging toward the boy, stepping inside his range, like Keven had done with him today at school. "See? It puts the opponent on the defensive, makes him veer away to get space for a strike." He left himself open enough for the boy to move in on him and get the feel of the maneuver.

"I don't know what Cheney meant about not having to prove yourself the winner," the boy said.

Troy was inclined to say, "I don't, either," but in this situation he was supposed to be the teacher. It was up to him to help convey the meaning. As the boy moved in on him again, he stepped away and clipped the boy a soft one to the side of the head. Again the boy attempted to step inside his range, and instead of stepping away, Troy rolled forward, sidestepped, and scored again.

126

"That's part of what it means," Troy said. "You are good, but I am better. I could wipe up this studio with you, but because I know I can, I don't have to."

Troy resumed letting the boy practice stepping inside his range. "I still don't get it," the boy said. "This doesn't count. We're not on the street."

The boy's words pulled a plug out of him, and into the space flowed the meaning of Cheney's words. But he didn't want to hear, didn't want to heed. The old karate maxim said: what you practice is what you do.

"But this does count," Troy said to the boy. "That's the point."

On the way to homeroom Friday morning, Troy saw Bert and Stuart dart down one stairway just as he came to the top of the other. The "point" from last night evaporated. With rage rising he sprinted across the hall and down the stairwell behind them. Their collars, the hairs of their heads, were just in reach at the bottom of the stairs when he saw Liesl and Donnie walk into the building. Liesl was wearing a patchwork blouse and a bright green skirt. Instantly his range of vision widened and he saw green as well as red.

This, he thought, is a choice. He drew his hand back from reaching out for Bert's neck and raised it to a wave as he called out, "Liesl."

She looked up, stopped, and Donnie Duggan walked on.

"Happy Cabrillo Day," he said as he approached her.

"On this day in . . . ?" she responded.

"Fifteen-forty-two," he filled in. "Juan Cabrillo, Portuguese navigator, discovered California."

"Oh!" she said, giving her books a squeeze. "I didn't know that, and I was born in California."

"I didn't know that," he said, mimicking the lilt of her voice. "I was born in Hanover."

"You and my mom," she said.

"And my dad," he said. "They went to school together, your mom and my dad. Did you know that?"

"Dear old Hanover Academy goes on forever."

"You sound as though you don't like it."

"Well, all the history gets a little thick," she said. "This town drips history like the oak trees drip Spanish moss. Parts of California have a similar history, the Spanish missions and all, but you don't have to validate yourself with your ancestors."

"Speaking of validate," he said, "I'd like to validate something for tomorrow. Confucius say stupid boy of yesterday would like to make amends for rudeness. Today is Confucius' birthday."

"On this date in. . . ?"

"Five-fifty-one B.C.," he said. "And tomorrow is the Festival of Gastronomy in Granby, Quebec. I can't afford to take you there, but how about a hamburger at noon at Lynch's? You can tell me about *Coppélia*."

Her grin of acceptance nearly made him go liquid but he managed to keep himself in solid form. "Where is your homeroom?" he asked, and he began walking her to it. "Tomorrow is also the birthday of Scotland Yard and the beginning of National Pickled Pepper Week," he said. He walked backward ahead of her so he could watch her eyes, her mouth, the hunch of her shoulders.

"Peter Piper picked a peck of pickled peppers," she began. The way she communicated with her shoulders was just one more thing he loved about her.

He left her at her homeroom door reluctantly. He wanted to grow to the spot, there by this door. Idly he wondered if it was too late for him to change

128

homerooms. But, no, he'd rather have her change homerooms and then he could have her and Miss Clutz both. Like in the hallway at the Rec Park building last Tuesday, he soared down the hall. Liesl wasn't holding his hand but she tethered him just the same. The full-whole-Troy-Matthews-feeling infused him. The "point" from last night reemerged. He didn't have to prove anything, he told himself. But what, then, would he do with dragoons and broken glass?

"May I talk to you?" he said to Miss Clutz as he came late to homeroom.

"How dire is it?" she asked. "I have a really pressed schedule today. Can it wait until after school?"

He wasn't sure he could manage the day. The program to kill was still roaring around inside, but since the dragoons were avoiding him, perhaps he could make it. He narrowed his focus purposely, determined to see green instead of red. He watched for that green skirt all day and didn't see it, not even in the cafeteria. He would have to find out her schedule. He was sure he could arrange to walk her to every class, no matter how fast he then had to run to his own. He stopped at the door of the choral room long enough to say, "Hi, Mom," but not long enough for her to even say, "Hi, Troy," back.

After school he told Miss Clutz about the dragoons and the broken glass, including the fact that no one else knew about it.

"Surely they will have to be made to fix it," she said, without the least suggestion that he should kill them afterward.

"But how can I make them do that?" he asked.

"I don't think you can," she said. "I think you need adult authority on your side. I suggest your father. I think you should tell your father about it."

129

All day he had been soaring, sailing, spinning, and now he was brought to earth like the proverbial lead balloon. Plunk. Talk to your father, she said.

"Yes, thank you, maybe so," he said, hiding his disappointment. Where were the miracle workers when you needed them? he wondered. He wanted *her* to have a solution. He wanted her to grab the dragoons by the hair and give them the justice due so he wouldn't have to do it. He didn't want to talk to his father.

As he left school he realized that Liesl lived nearby. Mr. Hutton had said they were neighbors. He walked across the back of the campus to Princess Avenue and down Princess until he came to Mr. Hutton's block. Yes, yes, of course, he thought as he saw the Duggans' house right next door to the Huttons'. He remembered now, remembered coming here with Dad when he was about nine years old. Looking through the telescope had been fascinating. He'd had a flurry of interest in astronomy and he had a feeling he was going to renew his interest.

He stalled on the sidewalk, wanting to go to the door and talk to Liesl about tomorrow. Was he supposed to come by here for her or meet her at Lynch's? The walkway that linked the public sidewalk, where he stood, to her front door was intimidating. He came out of his stall and briskly walked toward Duke Street. He would call her.

Thoughts of her almost pushed everything else out of his head. But when he walked into the house and saw Dad with photos spread out on the dining-room table, he remembered Miss Clutz's advice. Talk to your father. He exchanged greeting with his father and went to his room. Perhaps he should have talked to Cheney about it last night. After all, the problem between himself and the

130

dragoons was over karate, so at least Cheney was some-how involved. Dad wasn't involved at all. Until the blowup last Saturday Dad had had no interest in karate at all.

How would Dad feel, he wondered, if Troy never looked at the photos? Dad's pictures were framed and hung all over the house. Troy couldn't avoid them if he wanted to. He remembered Dad trying to interest him in photography and developing and he just wasn't inter-ested. That was about the same time he had the flurry of interest in astronomy. In spite of the fact that Troy wasn't interested in what Dad wanted him to be inter-ested in, Dad had taken him to the Duggans' to look through the telescope. Dad was eager to help Troy with whatever he was interested in.

Anything except karate. In spite of his philosophizing, the sting was still there. Dad had no interest in karate. Troy wondered if Dad had been stung by his own lack of interest in photography. The thought enlarged into in-sight. An "aha," as Mother called them. People who loved each other didn't necessarily have to have the same interests! The insight was so full and whole and real, he couldn't now imagine why he had been so repeatedly hurt by Mom's and Dad's disinterest in karate. It was more than disinterest. It was dislike. Yet they never told him he couldn't do it.

And Mom's music. Except for a short spurt of taking piano, he hadn't done anything with music, either. Darius was the one who was in honor chorus.

After musing a bit longer, he came out of his room and joined Dad in the dining room. He looked at the photo-graphs on the table. Hawks. Soaring hawks, hawks on wires, hawks at roost.

"Dad," Troy said. "I have a pretty serious problem and

131

I need to discuss it with you. I should have told you sooner." And he told.

Dad's ire was instant. His eyes were wide with indignation. "Who are these boys?" he asked.

Except for Dwight, Troy didn't even know their last names. But Dwight's was enough.

"Yes, I know his father. We went to school together. He's an accountant. A CPA."

Troy smiled, thinking of Liesl's comment about Hanover Academy going on forever.

Dad was at the phone and talking to Dwight's father in one minute, telling what had happened, saying Dwight, Stuart, and Bert should repair the glass. "No, tomorrow won't do," he said. "I think it should be done today. Right now. I'll be glad to pick up the boys and take them to get the glass and supervise the job, but it will have to be today."

Now Troy's eyes were wide. He'd never heard his father so adamant.

"Yes. Right. I'll wait here for your call." Dad turned to Troy. "He's going to see if he can round up the boys and talk to them. He'll call me back. I know you'd love to go watch and gloat, but I think you'd better stay right here. What do you think?"

Troy shrugged. Yes, he would love to go watch, but perhaps Dad was right. There'd been enough antagonism. His priorities had changed. Tomorrow there would be hamburgers at Lynch's with Liesl. He nodded agreement. The phone rang. Dwight's father had located the boys, and Dad was off.

14

*P*rincess Avenue had never looked more beautiful. The leaves of the evergreen live oaks made fine tracery against a crystal blue sky. And here was Liesl on the sidewalk.

His voice betrayed him. He talked in sprints and dashes as they walked down the street. He told her about coming to look through the telescope when he was nine, told about Harvey Hutton and doing cartoons for the paper, gave her the history of the founding of Georgia—Oglethorpe, not Cabrillo—and how this coastal area was the oldest part of the state.

"Peter Piper picked a peck of pickled peppers," she began.

For a bare moment he was startled at her interruption; then he caught her laughter and joined her.

"Uh, huh. You caught me validating!" he said. "But you have to admit, Grand Square is impressive." They crossed to Grand Square, angling to Lynch's, which was off the northwest corner of the square. Arms of oaks reached out to pull the town toward the square. Troy looked past Liesl to the southwest, toward the Ritz. He longed to see with his own eyes that the glass had been replaced as Dad said. He longed to see more than the one blob of caulk he had left on the glass.

"After lunch," he said, to make himself quit the history lesson, "I'll show you the Altamaha-ha."

"Oh," she said, "you mean that cartoon dragon you've drawn all over school? You've turned the whole school into Ha-has."

"Well, everyone needs a laugh," he said, wondering if she was laughing at him.

In Lynch's they sat in a booth about halfway down one side. There was also a center section of booths and a row of tables between the two sections. The high backs of the booths gave a sense of sanctuary.

"You can order anything you want," he said, "but they have the best hamburgers in town."

"Peter Piper picked a peck of pickled peppers," she said.

He looked at her, puzzled.

"I didn't just sprout yesterday," she said, smiling. "I've lived here for two years. I've even been in Lynch's before."

He nodded and smiled at himself in embarrassment.

She reached across the table and put her fingertips onto the knuckles of his left hand and he almost jerked back in reflex action. Before he moved, his brain shot out the message: Freeze! Electrical currents darted from her fingers and ran up his arm and the chill popped goose pimples onto the backs of his upper arms. Don't move, he commanded himself. Just don't move. With his free hand he picked up the menu and searched it as though he hadn't already decided what he would have to eat. "They have great Southern cooking here," he said, reading the menu to Liesl. "Turnip greens, chicken and dumplings, fried squash, chicken livers."

She looked at him intently and did not move her hand. "I can read too," she said.

How could she sit there so calmly? he wondered. How could she reach out and touch him so casually? Had she put herself on freeze too? He should have sat on the same side of the booth as she, he decided. At that thought an image sprang to mind of what else might be touching. He shivered and was grateful for the table in between.

The waitress plunked glasses of water and silverware on the table and palmed her tablet to take their order.

"I want a hamburger all the way and a large order of fries," he said. "And a Coke."

The waitress jotted down his order and looked at Liesl.

"The same," she said, "except make it a small order of fries. And some onion rings." She looked across at Troy. "Do you like onion rings? Will you share an order with me?"

He nodded and wondered if he should have given her order for her. Perhaps not. She might have said, "I know how to order."

During the ordering their hands had somehow become separated. He was both relieved and sorry. Now, how would he get her hand back?

"They have the best onion rings here," she said. Her remark made him feel absurd about the way he had acted like he was showing her around. "There are not many places you can get fresh-made onion rings anymore," she said.

Her black hair draped itself perfectly about her shoulders and her creamy, pale complexion made such a contrast that a lump came into his throat. He wished he'd never had the thought of sitting on the same side of the booth with her. All he could think of now was sitting next to her, with shoulders, arms, and thighs all touching. A dull ache pressed against his chest and, lower down, something else was pressing.

"How did you do with the dance history that you were working on?" he asked, thankful to his brain for giving

135

him the question. How did Darius do it? he wondered. Darius seemed as cool and casual as Liesl. Was it Molly who was the nervous and awkward one? Or was she, too, calm and casual? Darius had admitted that the feelings were scary. Troy didn't know what it was like to have a stroke, but he thought he might be having one.

Liesl told him a little about the dance-history project, then started talking about dance class. "Mrs. Thompson said she hated to press you but she really needs to know right away if you will be interested in coming to class and being Franz."

"What did you tell her?" he asked. The hamburgers were served and he took a huge, mouth-stuffing bite.

Liesl tilted her head and raised one shoulder toward it. She was so beautiful he thought he might faint. Or cry.

"I told her I hoped you would."

Internally he nearly hemorrhaged. How could he? Hadn't he enough trouble without adding the flak he'd get from going to dance class? His hands clung to the hamburger and he felt himself chew, chew, chew an endless wad. And there she sat looking at him with those sky-matching eyes. How could he not?

"*Coppélia* is a wonderful story," she said. "Or, rather, some parts of the story are wonderful. Ballet stories are often exaggeratedly romantic and dramatic and sometimes quite stupid. Like opera. But this one was written over a hundred years ago and there are automatons in it. I think you'll love it."

He knew he'd love it.

"Franz has a regular girlfriend. Me," she said. "But he falls in love with a girl he sees reading in a window and he doesn't know that she is simply a lifelike doll, the product of an inventor."

In between words they bit and chewed. Hamburgers,

136

french fries, onion rings. At this point, Troy couldn't be the one to prove that Lynch's hamburgers were the best in town. The hamburger, the french fries, the onion rings all tasted the same.

Afterward, before they went to Liesl's house to listen to the *Coppélia* music, they walked along the river. Troy summoned the Altamaha-ha, who answered the summons, and Liesl saw.

15

*O*ver the weekend, with the *Coppélia* music and Liesl dancing in his head, he drew the first of the political cartoons. Mr. Hutton wanted the high-forehead candidate spouting a quote about it being time for new ideas for Hanover. One of the man's best new ideas was to develop the waterfront. Hutton wanted an aside in the corner stating that developing the waterfront had been in the city-council minutes again and again for over sixty years.

After drawing it the traditional way, Troy had an inspiration. He redrew it, using the Altamaha-ha. Her long body formed the frame of the cartoon, the head meeting the tail in the upper-left corner. She overlooked the area of the cartoon and he had her make the comment about how long the development of the waterfront had been a new idea.

Monday morning he took both copies to the newspaper office. He walked along the river and the Ha-ha rose and frolicked along beside him. Whalelike, she dove and slapped her tail against the surface. Dragonlike, she came up spewing water instead of fire.

When he showed the Ha-ha cartoon to him, Mr. Hutton said, "Troy, this is great."

Troy chewed the inside of his lip to keep from grinning too much. The only word he could think of to describe his feelings on this Botswana Independence Day was "ecstasy." He wanted to do leaps, either karate or ballet. Liesl had showed him some more ballet movements on Saturday.

"It's been a dull week," Mr. Hutton said as Troy was leaving. "Why don't you go out and make some news?"

Troy laughed out loud and Mr. Hutton laughed back. "It's been a wonderful week," Troy said. He walked out of the office thinking he could make strange news. Boy dances down main street in Hanover, Georgia. He did manage to stay on the sidewalk and keep his feet to a normal pace, but in his imagination he was as frolicky as the Altamaha-ha.

At the Ritz corner, just as he turned his head to examine the glass, he was accosted by all three ragoos. All three of them put a hand to his chest and shoved him back into the alcove. When they had him thoroughly trapped in the corner, they stepped back and assumed the ready stance. All his muscles wanted to do likewise but, as when Liesl touched his hand at Lynch's Saturday, he told himself to freeze.

"What do you think you are, tall?" he said to Dwight.

"That smart-mouth stuff isn't going to work," Stuart said.

"And you, do you think you have curly hair?" Troy's mind was running faster than the digital tenths on a gas pump. There was the part of him who wanted to smash or be smashed. The adrenaline rush would make him capable of victory. But there was that other part that thought of Liesl and of what Dad said about choices. The ragoos, of course, might not allow him a choice. He wondered how serious they were. Their training to avoid a fray whenever possible was the same as his.

Incredibly, the *Coppélia* music was still cavorting in his

139

head. He took the spurt of the adrenaline and turned it into a run-through of ballet positions, complete with arm sweeps. The ragoos couldn't have been more surprised if his hair had suddenly turned purple.

With hands above his head, he executed the spinning turn Liesl had taught him Saturday. When he stopped revolving he leapt toward the three, who immediately parted so his leap carried him to the other side of the alcove. From there he could see the glass, whole and in place and complete with several small blobs of caulk. He gathered himself and leapt through again. He was astonished that they seemed totally defused. They did not raise hand, foot, or voice in kiai.

"Will that be all, gentlemen?" he said, making a deep, elaborate bow. While they still stood gaping, he stepped to the Clark Gable poster and gave Gable a parting kick to the nose. His toe did not overkick the mark. Then he walked straight across the street.

As soon as he stepped off the curb, he knew crossing the street was a wrong move. The way to school was across Grand Square. Once off the curb, though, he kept going as though he was sure of himself. On the other side, he looked back to see if they were registering and reacting to his mistake. They hadn't moved. They were not even chattering among themselves. If he was a king before, now he was a god. He gave them as supercilious a stare as it was possible to give from such a distance.

As though his contemptuous look had caused it, there was a sudden whumph of displaced air, felt more than heard. The sound was like one quick beat from an approaching helicopter, but it came from the Ritz.

The ragoos were heads-up and feet moving. The three bolted across to near where Troy stood and they stared back at the building. The building's old yellow bricks stood firm, but from within was the heavy sound of something huge sighing and giving way.

"The building's caving in," Bert said. There was a muffled sound of things falling.

Troy was the first to move. He darted to the *Historian* office and ran in yelling. "Mr. H., Mr. H., call the, uh . . . Something's just happened at the Ritz."

Mr. Hutton came running, ran past Troy and into the street, and looked toward the Ritz. "What? What?" he said to Troy, who had followed him out. The street was as still and quiet as it was any morning at eight A.M. Whatever had happened was over and there was no outward sign. But the three ragoos stood staring at the Ritz now, instead of at Troy.

"Something happened down there. The roof caved in or something," Troy said. He felt like Chicken Little saying the sky is falling, the sky is falling.

Mr. Hutton didn't question, even though there was nothing to see or hear. With Troy at his heels he ran back to the newspaper office and called the police.

Sirens were instantaneous. By the time Troy and Mr. Hutton were back on the sidewalk, wails filled the air and by the time they were on the corner standing across from the Ritz with the ragoos, a police car whirled in from one direction and a fire engine from another. Two policemen leapt from their car, firemen scurried down from the fire truck, and after all the great rush they stood back and looked. There was nothing to see.

"Get somebody down here with a key," said one of the firemen who had walked over and tried the door. "No use breaking in unless it's necessary." One of the policemen went to the patrol car and radioed a message. As though the street were normally lively at this hour, people began to appear from everywhere and fill the street.

141

"Tell them what you heard, Troy," Mr. Hutton said, stepping into the street beside the policemen and firemen.

"They heard it too," Troy said, including the ragoos. "We were practicing karate. They were showing me their candlestance."

"I thought the building was falling," Stuart said as the ragoos joined them in the street.

"I thought we were going to be buried in the rubble," Dwight said.

"We ran," Bert said. "And Troy ran for help." Bert gestured toward Troy, then to the building, which seemed to be just as intact as it had been yesterday and all the yesterdays before.

The crowd held a collective breath when the doors were unlocked and two of the firemen cautiously pushed them open. The two men disappeared into the bowels of the building but were back in less than a minute.

"The roof's fallen in," one said. "The place is a wreck."

"Soaking wet, too," the other said. "That roof must have been collecting water for ages."

"Must have," a policeman said. "It hasn't rained for weeks."

Murmured relief broke through the crowd, that the firemen had emerged safely, that things were no worse than they were.

One of the policemen sidled up to Troy. "I know a little karate," he said, "but what is a candlestance?"

"A move that is like a candle," he said, thinking fast. "As quick as the flicker of a flame." The man didn't question that a stance is not a movement and Troy didn't dare look at the ragoos.

"Hey, look, man," Bert said, sounding just like Keven.

Troy looked, mind fleeting to ward off Bert's objection to the flippant remark.

142

"Not here, there," Bert said, pointing. Troy, as well as Dwight and Stuart, followed the exact course of Bert's direction. He was pointing at the Ritz. The glass, which they'd all had a hand in replacing, was whole and intact.

"Maybe we should celebrate by going to the Okra Strut Ball in Irmo, South Carolina."

The ragoos looked at Troy and all three said, "What?"

"Well, I asked you for some news, Troy," said Mr. Hutton, "but don't you think this was a little melodramatic?"

16

*B*etween the excitement of the roof cave-in and the excitement of Liesl, karate class faded to the background of his mind.

Everyone treated him like a hero just because he had been on the spot when the Ritz roof caved in. The attitude puzzled Troy. He had done nothing to warrant such attention. He hadn't been Superman and held the roof up while someone escaped without injury.

In karate class, Cheney had them do parts of the demonstration for the class. The routines clicked smoothly even though they were ad-libbing Nick into it as they went along. The classmates roared with pleasure. This attention was at least earned, but somehow it made Troy uncomfortable just the same. But he didn't think about it. His mind-time was moving toward Tuesday. Liesl's dance class was Tuesday night.

Not knowing what else to wear to ballet class, he wore his gi. Liesl had said, "Wear something loose," which made him wonder at the strange use of words. He knew what she meant. Clothing which allowed free bodily movement was "loose." But they called theirs "tights"!

He refused to think ahead to when he himself might be wearing tights. Every ounce of his mental and physical energy would be required just to walk into the dance studio. He thought only of Liesl and those small angular shoulders and the sapphire eyes.

She met him on the steps of the Rec building, her whole face shining at the sight of him. Maybe her whole body was shining. He knew his was.

"This is Troy Matthews," Liesl said, introducing him to the class of leotarded dancers. "He's going to be Franz." The shouts went up just like at karate class last night. Each raised voice, each pair of clapping hands fired darts of self-consciousness into him. He smiled and mentally dropped all his body weight to his feet to keep him from fleeing as he had last week. He was stunned at the thought it was only last week he'd had the first shock of this glaring, mirrored room. How could so much life happen in just one week?

"Is that your karate uniform?" a girl asked.

"Well, we don't call it a uniform," he said. "It's a gi."

"What belt is that?" another asked.

"Well," he said, looking down at his brown belt. "It's the belt just before black belt."

"Ooooh," some of the girls said.

"I can see we're not going to settle down to ballet until we hear a little about karate," Mrs. Thompson said. "Troy, will you show us some techniques? Why don't you do one of your katas?"

The room suddenly became more comfortable. Most people didn't even know what a kata was, and she not only knew but also knew he wouldn't have his brown belt unless he knew some. Well, katas were his meat. He stood at ready, then began the rhythmic series of punches and kicks and his body relaxed. The kinks unkinked and the threat disappeared from the room. If he could do karate here, he could dance here. The applause bounded off the walls and he didn't feel so attacked, but it still bothered him. As they started the warm-up exercises, he thought about it. How could applause feel like an attack, anyway? Because of embarrassment? Because of having done nothing to earn that first burst except walk into the room and be introduced? At the same time there was warmth in it. He'd known for a long time he was a person who liked attention. That was one of the reasons he'd developed his calendar tricks.

With his foot on the bar, he copied the girls in extending his arms and curving his body forward until he was stretched out along his leg. Soon, mind as well as muscle was mesmerized by movement.

"You're a natural," Mrs. Thompson said. "You could really be good."

He smiled acknowledgment of her comment and wondered how many people it was possible to love. She hadn't said, as many people would have, "You *are* good." And yet he was good, he knew, for a rank beginner in ballet. The sign of the talent was there. But he fully understood that she spoke as a dancer and that being good as a dancer was achieved only through work, the same as karate. He knew better than to think that a plié and a pirouette were ballet, any more than a kiai and a karate chop were karate. His eyes sought out Liesl at the opposite bar. She seemed totally lost to the dance, and he liked that too.

After stretching, they herded onto the auditorium stage to block the first scene. It involved Troy, as Franz, wandering back and forth across the stage, which was to become a village, and looking lovesick toward the girl in the window. Looking lovesick was one of the easiest things he'd ever done.

Not knowing Liesl had taught him on Saturday, Mrs. Thompson showed him how to do the spinning turns. His outward kick propelled him, one kick per turn. He had been most interested, when Liesl had told him, in the fact that a dancer kept head straight, eyes front, and moved it in a quick snap to keep from getting dizzy. These turns would work wonderfully into a kata routine, he thought.

"Now, let's see if we can get you to catch Liesl and lift her to your shoulder," Mrs. Thompson said.

The idea made Troy dizzier than the spinning had. What if he dropped her? But Mrs. Thompson showed him how to scoop Liesl as she jumped, so it would look like he was catching and lifting when, mainly, he would be supporting and guiding, using her momentum. He understood that. In karate you used the other person's momentum instead of fighting against it. With Mrs. Thompson coaching, they went through several dry runs, Liesl running toward him with such delicate steps. He'd shouldered and thrown many boys in karate class, yet he was afraid this small girl might knock him over. How awful, if they went sprawling.

Here she came, in the tiptoed run, and he reached for her waist, and her body rose, turned slightly in his hands, and she was on his shoulder. He was surprised at how small she felt, and how strong. Such a muscular body beneath his fingertips. Mrs. Thompson clapped. He was glad his face was already red from the spinning. All he could think of was Saturday in the booth at Lynch's and how many body parts were now touching.

"You catch on quickly," Mrs. Thompson said when he'd become adept at catching and lifting. "Now brace yourself while she lowers herself headfirst. Go on, Liesl. I'm right here."

He felt Liesl's leg muscles tighten and she flowed backward and draped herself to the floor. Hands to floor, she arched her legs and turned herself aright.

"Troy, I could get to like you," Mrs. Thompson said. "I've never had anyone from Hanover who could do this.

147

And most fourteen-year-olds, even if they were interested, aren't strong enough."

"Karate," he said, flexing his arm. He had no idea what else to say, but he wanted to say something.

They continued practicing leaps and turns and scooping Liesl to his shoulder until finally it didn't matter at all that this was Liesl he was touching. The buoyancy of his body was so exhilarating that it was only he, himself, Troy, dancing and enjoying the dance.

"You haven't told me what day this is," Liesl said while Mrs. Thompson was busy with the chorus of future villagers.

Already anticipating that rise of her shoulders and her "On this date in . . . ?" response, he grinned and said, "This is Phileas Fogg's Wager Day."

17

On Thursday, the anniversary of *Sputnik,* he was launched into apprehension over the karate demonstration for the muscular-dystrophy kids. He couldn't envision where it would take place, although Cheney had said it would be outside if the weather was good. In Hanover in October the weather was seldom anything but pure perfection. It was Troy's favorite time of year.

He couldn't envision the kids, either, and that somehow nagged at him. He wanted to see their faces and get a feel for them. Dad agreed to take him over.

As they drove toward the River Bridge, Troy stared blankly out the window, not seeing the marsh, the bridge, the soaring gulls until Dad spoke.

"Wouldn't it be great to be a gull for a while?"

Troy turned his blank gaze to his father, then looked out the window and saw. Gulls were gliding the thermals above the bridge.

"Air surfers," Troy said.

"What a great description," Dad said. "May I use that as a caption?"

What thermals had he been riding in his own interior? he wondered. Dragoons, Nick, Keven, Liesl, these kids? Even as he wondered, he knew. Fear. He was afraid he would not measure up. When he shook it off by trying to think of the kids, he was embarrassed to have a full,

149

whole body when they did not. A tingling sensation moved along his arms and when he looked, the hair was rising. Relax, relax, he told himself. It's not going to be that bad. They're just kids. He forced himself to think he was a gull, above everything looking down.

"On the way back, I'm going to stop at the rookery," Dad said.

"Mmmm," Troy murmured. He couldn't think rookery, stopping, or anything else at the moment.

As they drove between the stone pillars of Crab Creek Campground, Troy's eyes were roving. The first kid he saw was being pushed in a wheelchair. The boy's head thrust back from an overprominent chest, and arms and hands were drawn awkwardly to the chest. Dreadfully thin legs dangled out from khaki multipocketed shorts. Troy felt like someone had just grabbed a fistful of his guts.

Abruptly Dad pulled to the side. Coming at them were four wheelchairs abreast, being pushed on the run, chair occupants shouting and hollering.

"What are they doing?" Troy asked.

"Looks like wheelchair races to me," Dad said.

"Wheelchair races!" Troy was appalled. Behind the four abreast came another four, these wheeling themselves, hands and arms darting back and forth to propel the chairs. How could they make fun of it like that? Troy wondered.

In the parking area there was a truck loaded with hay.

"Wonderful," Dad said. "They're going to have a hayride."

"Nah. That's for someone else," Troy said. Crab Creek was a large complex and usually had several things going on at once. As they stepped into the parking lot Dad spoke to a boy wheeling himself along. "Who's having a hayride?"

150

"We are," the boy said with enthusiasm.

Troy watched the boy roll away. A small delight was rising, chasing out the fear. Imagine them having wheelchair races and going on hayrides! Even when something this awful was happening to you, he guessed you couldn't bear to be sad all the time.

None of the camp directors were around but someone pointed to where the demonstration would probably be and Troy and Dad wandered out among the oaks. Two boys were tussling on the soft grass.

"Counselor's children," Troy commented.

"No, I don't think so," Dad said.

"But . . ." He didn't finish the sentence. These boys were all right. They looked and acted physically fine.

"This is a disease that can sometimes be detected before there are any physical signs."

Something gripped Troy's gut again. "But why would they come? Why would their parents let them come?" The idea of these two healthy-looking boys seeing into their gnarled future was piercing.

Dad shrugged. They began wandering back toward the car and the campers began gathering around the porch of the dining hall. "I guess so they can see that even though this is what is going to happen to them, they can still have some fun and enjoy life. They need to know that as long as life lasts, life *is*."

Near the car there was a small dark-haired girl being rolled along and Troy had the tingling sensation again. She will never be a dancer, he thought. Two other campers passed, heading toward the dining hall. One was being wheeled, the other was wheeling himself with a counselor following behind.

"We're having a karate demonstration tomorrow, did you know that?" one boy said.

"Yeah," said the other. "I can hardly wait."

151

Dad looked at Troy and winked.

On the return trip Troy was more pensive than before. He thought he was such a hotshot, so tough. He wondered how tough he'd be if he had something like muscular dystrophy.

At the rookery Dad set the camera on the tripod.

"Don't forget, it's karate night," Troy said, knowing he was in for a siege. He hadn't been here with Dad since he was old enough to say he didn't care a thing about watching birds fly in to roost.

"Here comes a snowy," Dad said. "Come on, get out and look. There won't be many. It's too early yet."

Troy stayed put in the car. Not only did he still not care about the birds, he had just seen too much to switch it off. In a moment, though, he did turn his head and look out. There was a dark speck in the distance. He watched the dark bird as it enlarged, gained a different perspective of light, and became a white bird. The snowy egret. How had Dad known it was a snowy?

In another moment he could make out the yellow feet, which dangled behind, then lowered for a landing. The bird hit and grasped a limb, wings afloat like sails, then folding. Within ten seconds of the lowering of the feet the bird was perched, neck doubled down on itself, looking not like a bird at all but like a huge magnolia blossom. The gracefulness of the bird reminded him of Liesl, and the thought of her removed him one bit more from the camp kids. But thoughts of her also reminded him of karate class, where he would be in a few minutes. And he wondered how long before his friends found out what he was doing on Tuesday nights. The thought made him cringe.

"Here come the ibis," Dad said, and Troy looked up and watched the three large birds, white with black-trimmed wings. A long bill curved downward at the front and the trailing legs made a similar curve at the rear. Troy smiled and stepped from the car.

"The Studebaker bird," he said, pleased to remember Dad's name for the bird. When Dad was a boy there had been an automobile called Studebaker and one year they'd come out with a startling bullet-nosed design which was almost the same, front and back. There had been jokes, Dad said, about not knowing if a Studebaker was coming or going. The ibis lowered their landing gear and two landed awkwardly but without much fluttering for balance. The third couldn't gain his balance and flapped and flew to another limb, tried and failed, and fluttered to yet a third spot before he was able to settle.

"I didn't know they ever had trouble alighting," Troy said.

"Oh, sure," Dad said, taking down his camera equipment. "Birds have different degrees of grace, just like humans do."

Troy scanned the sky. There were no more dark specks at the moment. Later, he knew, there would be the larger yellow-billed American egrets, Louisiana herons, green herons, great blue herons and little blue, the short-necked yellow-crested and black-crested night herons, and sundry grackles and red-winged blackbirds. He was surprised at the accurate return of his memory from when he was younger and Dad pointed out the birds to him incessantly.

"There's the first rabbit," Dad said as they drove along the causeway back toward Hanover. "Do you remember the bunny counts?"

"Of course," Troy said.

"There's two," Dad said. "Three, four, five."

"One, two," Troy said when he saw rabbits on his side.

153

"I guess I learned to count by counting marsh rabbits. Three." The rabbits came to the edge of the marsh to feed, morning and evenings. Dad was up to forty-seven and Troy to forty-four as they approached the River Bridge.

As they started up the incline, the red lights flashed and the barriers began to lower.

"Good," said Dad and Troy at the same time. They looked at one another and grinned. They were the first car up to the barrier and they got out of the car and looked up and down the river for whatever boat was coming. Sometimes there were freighters, sometimes sailboats whose masts were too tall for the unopened structure. At high tide, the shrimp boats, too, needed the bridge to rise so they could pass under.

"It's that freighter just leaving the dock," Dad said.

One of Troy's lifetime treats had been this river and the river traffic. He had grown up with Dad saying, "Let's go," almost every time they heard a ship's whistle signal to the bridge-tender. They'd hop in the car and ride to the bridge just to stop and watch the ships go under, and they talked and dreamed about where the ship had been or where it was going and what language the crew spoke.

Troy watched the elevator span rise between the towers and marveled at the ingenuity which brought forth this particular combination of concrete and steel.

"Hey, Goose," someone called. Troy turned and saw that Nick and Keven had pulled up to the barrier in the lane next to Dad. Keven pounded on the side of the car and Troy walked over. Other cars were rolling to a stop on the bridge now.

As he walked over, he thought of Liesl and ballet and that Keven and Nick would be hardest on him about it.

What better place, he thought, to tell them about it, when even if they raucously teased him, there would be no one else to hear, and perhaps by class time they would have adjusted a little. There was no way to say it gracefully, no way to sneak up on it and inject it casually into a conversation.

"I have the boards in the trunk," Nick said.

"Mmm," Troy said. There was nothing special about the boards, just a length of lumber cut in one-foot sections, for them to play macho board-breakers. But Troy was distracted, so he just plunged in.

"I want to tell you guys something I've been doing," he began.

"Hey, yeah, man. What now?" Keven talked across Nick to where Troy stood on the driver's side. "You've seen another sea monster?"

"Well, something just as surprising," Troy said, grateful to at least have something to bounce off. "I'm going to ballet class."

"What?" Keven said. "Say that again. I thought I heard you say you were going to ballet class."

"You heard it right," Troy said, glancing over his shoulder at Dad at the rail across the bridge. The freighter was just easing away from the upriver dock. Progress toward the bridge was quick enough so that the ships didn't depart the dock until the bridge span was up. Troy realized his parents didn't even know about the ballet class yet. Perhaps he should have told them first, but it was too late now.

"Ballet! What are you doing at ballet class?" Keven asked.

Troy could tell from Keven's tone that he didn't suspect dancing. Did Keven think he was designing scenery, or teaching them karate, or what? He threw one arm

155

forward and one back and lifted one leg up and back in an arabesque.

"Dancing," he said.

"Hey, come on, man," Keven said. "That's carrying the Liesl bit a little too far."

"Liesl?" Troy said. "What do you know about Liesl?"

"Oh, come on, man, do you think I'm blind?"

Troy's breath quickened. His brain flicked about for a statement of denial but he found none.

"Troy!" he heard Dad call out from across the bridge. Without looking, he waved a just-a-minute hand behind him. Troy didn't realize that Nick had not said anything until he did say something.

"Your old dad went to ballet class a couple of times years ago," Nick said.

"What?" Troy said. Nick had turned his head slightly toward Keven.

"Yup," Nick said, nodding his head several times before he continued. "Same reason. A girl."

Keven groaned.

"How do you like it?" Nick asked.

Aspersions rolled around in Troy's throat, excuses, words to imply he didn't really like it but that Liesl had somehow pressured him into it. But he stopped them at the back of his tongue, and out popped the truth. "I love it," he said.

Keven clutched his stomach as though in physical pain.

They almost didn't hear Nick say, "Me too."

"Troy! Troy!" Dad called again.

"Yup," Nick said. "I really liked it and that scared me silly. I went twice and didn't go back. I wasn't as sure of myself at fourteen as you are, Troy."

"Sure of myself?" Troy said. "Sure of myself?" If all this agony had been from being sure of himself, he would hate to have been unsure.

"I'm really proud of you," Nick said.

"And I think I'm going to barf," said Keven.

"Troy, Nick, Keven," came Dad's insistent voice. Troy turned to see Dad running toward them. "Run," Dad said. "Run. The ship is going to hit the bridge."

Troy was already looking upriver, toward Dad, beyond Dad. The ship was a thousand yards away, slightly south of the usual course but with enough time to make a correction.

Nick raised up in his seat and looked.

"It has plenty of time," Troy said. The bridge had been built at a curve of the river and ships leaving dock made a dog-leg turn for the bridge.

"No," Dad said. "No, it hasn't. It should have made the turn already. It will hit the bridge."

Troy rolled his eyes. Dad was not ordinarily overly dramatic. Why pick now? He'd just given Keven and Nick enough to absorb. Even now, he saw, the ship was turning. "See," he said. "It's turning. It's turning."

Dad shook his head and as Troy shook his own back, Dad gripped his upper arm. "It's making the turn too late. Let's get out of here."

Troy sighed. His chicken father was going to play Chicken Little and run shouting, "The bridge is falling, the bridge is falling." Why? Why now when they had been so close to being close?

"Get ahold of yourself, man," Nick said.

"Run," Dad repeated, jerking Troy off balance and shoving him down the bridge. "Run. I'll warn the others." Dad ran along to the next two cars, yelling, "Get out and run. The ship is going to hit the bridge."

Troy closed his eyes in humiliation. The ship was still several hundred yards away. It did look huge and close, but they always did. He wanted to melt away like a salted snail. Instead, he ran, not the obedient son but the embarrassed one. He ran a few steps and looked back, ran a few steps and looked back.

As Dad moved down the line of traffic, people rolled up their car windows to protect themselves from the crazy man. On top of his taking ballet, Troy thought, Keven would never let him live this down. He ran down the bridge holding his stomach as Keven had so recently done. "No, no, no," he cried out into the wind.

Then in one glance, his "no" changed meaning.

The ship was at the side of the bridge nosing through the railing as though into a marshmallow. Dad was still running along the line of cars, shouting and knocking on windows. No one, no one at all, had left the security of a car to follow.

"Da-a-a-ad!" Troy screamed. "Run, Dad." He ran back up the bridge, grabbed Dad's hand, and they ran backward, backward away from the ship that was plowing through the bridge as easily as through a wave. A wake of steel and concrete sprayed into the air and the side of the bridge toward which the ship was plunging fell away, east, into the water, dropping cars, cars full of people, out into space and down into the water. The noise of the collapsing structure and the screams was horrendous but Troy didn't hear a sound. He and Dad ran back and back and back and the rupture of the bridge stopped at their feet.

Their car and the car with Keven and Nick were the first to disappear.

18

*T*he first moment on the safe span, while the bridge was still falling, Troy thought Dad had panicked, because he kept on running. Troy ran after, still screaming and not hearing his own voice. Even worse than standing on the crumpling bridge with Dad would be standing there alone, alone.

Near the bottom of the bridge Dad leapt the railing and ran through the marsh. Troy wanted to call him back. All that falling debris would create a whirlpool, he thought, and suction the marsh—and Dad—into the water. Even so, he ran after, needing to be with Dad, near Dad.

"Come on, son, help me," Dad called back into the thundering silence. "I've found someone."

The water was as turbulent as if lashed by storm. From somewhere beneath his toenails Troy dredged up his training, his karate calm. Halfway through the bridge, the ship stuck and loomed. The churning water loomed. At the edge of the water someone was floundering. Dad reached him, then Troy, dragging the person out.

"Dad, it's Nick. It's Nick." Troy's voice knew no volume but high. It was Nick and Nick was alive! They dragged him into the marsh.

In the water nearby was someone else, clinging to some floating debris. Dad splashed into the water to

159

help. Troy was too afraid to go into the water but he reached out as soon as they were close enough. A woman was clinging so fiercely to a car seat that they had to drag it as well as her into the marsh.

"It's all right now," Dad said quietly. "It's all right."

"It's all right now, it's all right," Troy screamed.

Dad reached out and touched Troy's arm and signaled, "Shhh."

The touch, the signal, made Troy realize he was shaking and jerking, about to jump out of his skin, and that his voice had been leaping out of his throat. The woman kept crying someone's name, and Nick, in the nearby marsh, was sobbing and calling for Keven.

Keven. Where was Keven? "Keve-e-e-en!" Troy called. Where was Keven? His eyes searched frantically across the water, which was now mostly level and still.

In minutes or millennia a shrimp boat plucked them from the edge of the marsh and took them across the river. Everyone was in a calm, efficient panic. Dad could not make them understand that he and Troy had not gone down with the bridge. Along with Nick and the woman they were shepherded into an ambulance, the woman finally being parted from the car seat, which she had not relinquished even when hauled aboard the shrimp boat.

Nick continued to cry for Keven.

"Wait and see," Dad said, meaning to be encouraging. "Perhaps he's all right."

Troy didn't believe it, but he was too numb to cry. If Keven was all right, he would have been in the same area of the river as Nick. Keven was not all right. Keven was at the bottom of the river, buried in concrete, steel, and seawater.

The hospital emergency room was all chrome and

160

chaos. Ambulances were coming and going without sirens or flashing lights. "We don't want to alarm the community," someone said. Injuries were being tended, though, amazingly, most of those brought in were not badly injured. Names and addresses were being taken and Dad finally made it clear they had not gone down with the bridge, although their car had. "We want you to stay and let us be sure you're not in shock," a nurse said.

They were staying, anyway. Staying with Nick, waiting, waiting, to hear something about Keven.

"Have they brought in a boy, a fourteen-year-old boy?" Dad asked periodically.

"No, no, I'm sorry. There's a girl about that age."

Troy's heart leapt. Liesl!

"Her name is Ann Harris."

His heart kept on jumping. Keven, Keven.

The waiting room became a mélange of people searching for their loved ones. There were some whose search was hopeless. One young couple reunited with hugs of thanksgiving. Each had thought the other dead. Some were dead. No one knew yet how many. Dad kept an arm around Troy's shoulder, keeping him close. Somewhere along the way, he called Mother.

"I just taught her to swim," the young man said. "We had our first argument over it." They'd been on their honeymoon in Florida and he had been insistent that she learn to swim. Swimming, it turned out, was what had saved her.

Another ambulance came rolling in, and incredibly, here came Keven, walking on his own, not crying but breathing in grief-stricken hunks.

Dad saw him first and called his name.

"Mr. Matthews, Mr. Matthews!" Keven saw Dad and ran to him and crashed into his chest to be held.

161

"Your dad's right here," Dad said. "He's all right. Nick, here's Keven. He's safe."

The two hugged and hugged and hugged. Every few seconds they stood back at arm's length to look and see that it was really true.

"How did you get out of the car? How did you get ashore? Are you really all right?" Questions, answers, and assurances swarmed about them.

In the end there were those who didn't find their loved ones. Seven cars filled with twenty-four people had gone down. Only seventeen came back up alive. Ann Harris, who was in eighth grade at Hanover Junior High, had lost her entire family.

19

And there was still the karate demonstration for the muscular-dystrophy kids.

"We can take Mom's car," Troy said when Mom had driven them home. The burgundy Mercedes and Dad's copper-colored Maverick were at the bottom of the river flowing out to sea.

"Yes, I guess we'll have to for a while," Dad said. All this had happened and they were home by ten o'clock.

"I mean to get to the demonstration," Troy said.

"Oh, son, you don't have to do that. We'll call them. They won't expect you to come."

"Those kids are counting on it," Troy said.

"I know, I know, sweetheart," Mother said, "but they'll understand."

"But I want to. The kids are counting on it. Darius and I can do it." Remembering those kids in the light of what had happened somehow made it even more important. "I have to," he said.

"Okay," Dad said. "Okay."

So it was that the alarm clock screeched him awake when he didn't know he'd fallen asleep. He had the hit-by-a-truck syndrome and was as disoriented and stiff as if he had fallen from the bridge. Grief for Keven sprang to his chest before he could remind himself that Keven was okay.

"You don't have to go," Dad said. "We'll call them."

"I have to," Troy said. His skein of thoughts was as tangled as though it had been played with by a kitten. Or mauled by a lion. He couldn't say why he had to go. But those kids haunted him and were all mixed up with the tumbling bridge.

Troy didn't even notice that Dad had left the house until he returned. "I just put your boards in the car," Dad said.

"The boards?" His head whirled. He'd forgotten the breaking boards. His gut wrenched. They were at the bottom of the river in the trunk of the Mercedes. How had Dad . . . ? "How?" he asked.

"Harvey Hutton zipped them off on his table saw," Dad said.

"Oh," Troy said. Then, "How?" again, meaning how had Mr. Hutton gotten into it, and how had Dad known he needed boards?

"Dragged him out of bed too. He'd been up all night. But I couldn't think of anyone else with a table saw."

Hairs prickled on the back of Troy's neck, that Dad would . . . that Mr. Hutton would . . . when he himself had forgotten.

Mother came too, and they drove by for Darius. Troy expected a barrage of questions about the bridge but Darius said nothing about it. They had to drive umpteen miles inland and loop back out to get to the Golden Isle causeway. Then Darius asked, "Why are we going this way?"

"You didn't hear about the bridge last night?"

"No, what about the bridge?"

"It got knocked out."

"Did the Altamaha-ha eat it?"

"I'm serious."

164

"You, serious?"

"He's serious," Mother said from the front seat.

"How come you think Mom and Dad are taking us instead of Keven and Nick?"

"Yeah, sure, come to think of it. How come?"

Troy and Dad told about being on the bridge, but neither of them said much. It was all still logjammed inside. Troy knew Keven was safe, but that first raw shock of thinking he was dead was still in him. After the initial burst of chatter, all conversation ceased, and they were looking for the bridge long before it came in view. As they approached the causeway, with the bridge and Hanover to the north, they gaped at the three-hundred-foot gap in the mile-long bridge.

"It's a wonder the whole thing didn't topple," Mother said. The standing part of the bridge seemed to be un-damaged and sturdy, each section on its own pilings as though the bridge was simply unfinished, waiting for the remaining sections to be put into place.

"Good construction," Dad said.

"Wow," said Darius. "Wow. You must feel like a hero, Mr. Matthews."

"No," Dad said, "I don't. If anyone had listened to me and run clear, I might."

Troy winced. He had been one of the ones who hadn't listened. Only sheer embarrassment had moved him down the bridge.

"I think he's a hero," Mom said, ruffling the back of Dad's hair.

"Me too," Troy said, and they were silent again for a mile or so.

"Well, we have to decide what we're going to do, how we're going to handle things without Keven and Nick," Troy said, and they began chattering and improvising.

When they arrived at Crab Creek they found the director and let him know they were there.

"Yes, I'm especially glad to see you. I wondered if you'd get over, with the bridge out. Terrible thing. But I'm glad you're here. The kids are really looking forward to it."

Troy didn't say anything about being on the bridge, and Mother, Dad, and Darius took the cue. He'd had more attention than he could bear for one week.

They rehearsed briefly on the lawn under the ancient oaks, Troy taking the bully part and Darius dispatching him forthrightly. Then the kids began gathering. Some were walking as though there was nothing the matter, some were limping or bobbing, some were on crutches and some in wheelchairs propelling themselves, and others, with distorted, folded-over bodies, were in wheelchairs being pushed.

"Hey, I saw you over here last night," a boy said to Troy. "Are you one of the karate people?"

"I am indeed," Troy said. "Put 'er there." He held out his hand and shook hands with the boy.

As the group gathered in a ragged semicircle, Troy and Darius sat in front of them meditating.

"Let me know when you're ready," the camp director whispered.

"We're ready," Troy said, and he was ready. He had meditated the bridge away. The camp director expressed appreciation for their being there and said he'd let them introduce themselves. Troy stood up and began.

"My name is Troy," he said, "and this is Darius. We're from Cheney's Karate Studio. You may think that as you were coming and getting into place, waiting for us to begin, we were merely sitting here waiting to start. Not so. The martial arts are mental as well as physical. We were meditating, preparing our minds.

166

"I don't know how much you know about the martial arts. Who can tell me what they are?" He looked out at the kids and called on them as they raised their hands.

"Self-defense," said one.

"Judo."

"Karate."

"Jujitsu."

"Bruce Lee."

"Chuck Norris."

"Joe Corley."

Troy laughed. "Now, there's a person who really knows karate," he said at the mention of Atlanta's Joe Corley. "Real karate, not just movies. Now, after we meditate, we do some exercises to warm up. I'll bet all of you do warm-up exercises too, right?"

A chorus of "rights" bellowed up and hung there under the trees. What did they think when he said that, he wondered, these kids with the deteriorating muscles? "You can't expect to do a flying sidekick"—he did one, snapping the leg of his gi as he did—"if you haven't warmed up. We, by the way, have already warmed up, though we'll show you some of our warm-up exercises in a minute. Even I can't do a good flying sidekick without warming up. You might split something you didn't intend to split." There was laughter. "And I don't mean your pants." More laughter. He and Darius moved through a shortened sequence of stretching exercises. Darius stayed with him so exactly that they looked like . . . well, dancers.

"This outfit we're wearing is called a gi," Troy said when they'd finished the stretching exercises. "It is for no other purpose than to be loose-fitting enough to allow movement in any direction. Darius?" Darius moved in all directions, using a bit from his kata. A chorus of "wows" fluttered like butterflies.

"And the belts. Let me tell you a little about the belts."
He wished, wished, wished he had his black belt, but it
was still only brown. "The belts are an indication of the
level of skill and progress, just like the grade you are in at
school." He wanted to bite his tongue. Were they all in
school? Were they able to go to school? He shrugged it
off to enable himself to continue. If he became too self-
conscious he would goof up and not be able to give them
his best.

"Karate is a very old system of the martial arts and it
was patterned after the defenses used by animals such as
the tiger." He made a fast catlike swipe with his hand.

"Or a leopard."

Darius looked wary and stalked. The two alternated
expressing the movements of dragon, snake, and crane.
For the crane, Troy drew his arms and shoulders up,
back, and out like the extended wings of a crane. Then he
drew his right arm slowly to his chest and darted it out
with a stiff open hand, like a beak. There was more
laughter and applause.

"Back to the belts," he said, realizing he'd gotten off
track. "You may be interested to know the reason the
belts first came into existence. The martial artists in the
Philippines wore white baggy breeches and they simply
tied a white rope around their waists to keep their pants
up." Giggles sprinkled through the group. "True. It's all
true," he said, hitching at his own pants as though they
might fall.

These kids were hanging on every word. He'd heard
entertainers say they could tell when the audience was
with them and now he knew what they meant. Everyone
was with him. "And if Darius had been a martial artist for
a long time and I had just started, guess what? His belt
would be dingy and dirty and mine would be . . . ?" He
waggled his fingers to summon a response.

168

"Clean."

"White."

"There are different types of martial arts and different styles in each type, and some of them use a different color system of belts. For instance, we use white, purple"—he pointed to Darius—"blue, green, brown, and black. But always, no matter what the style, the lightest belt is for the beginner and the darkest, black, for the most proficient."

He saw Cheney appear at the back of the crowd and lean against a tree. A current of nervousness rippled through him but he told himself to relax and pretend Cheney was not there.

"There are two things we do in karate. One is called the kata, which is just a stylized routine of forms. The other is learning self-defense. We will show you both. First, Darius will do a kata he has worked out for himself." In fact, Troy had also worked out his own kata, and had incorporated some of the ballet kicks and spins into it. He was thinking he might enter the form competition at the tournament tomorrow.

Troy was amazed at how much Darius had improved. Cheney's ultimatum had had its effect. Or was it because there were no judges here? The children were not judging. They were only enjoying. Even without the music, Darius executed the kata beautifully. Troy knew that Darius heard the music in his head, that music, not karate, was his passion. He had a passion for karate only when music was involved. As Darius spun and punched and kicked, Troy gave up his investment in having Darius as absorbed in karate as he himself was. The audience was so spellbound that it was a full ten seconds after Darius stopped before they began to applaud.

"I didn't know karate was dancing," Troy heard a little girl say. He grinned. He hadn't known it long himself.

"Next we'll have a demonstration of breaking boards." Breaking boards was, really, a House of Dragons sort of performance trick, but Cheney taught it so his students would do it right and not hurt themselves. "How many of you have seen exhibitions, perhaps on television, where they break boards or concrete blocks or bricks?" A few random affirmations were uttered. "Before we do this, I want you to understand that we didn't just start breaking boards. We didn't just say one day, I think I'll break some boards. We've had a lot of training and practice. If you try to break a board without the proper training, what you'll break is your hand," he said. "In other words, don't do it." His favorite karate cartoon, from one of the magazines, was of a guy who'd just karate-chopped a brick and he was left with the rectangular imprint in his hand.

"The breaking of boards has no real value except to demonstrate the strength and thrust of the blow." He didn't tell them that, actually, it was rather easy to do as long as the blow was with the grain of the wood and not against it. He also did not tell them that martial artists practiced on boards in lieu of breastbones. And he didn't look at his parents, who understood and hated this symbolism. They had never watched and he didn't want to know whether or not they were watching now.

Harder than breaking boards was holding the board while someone else broke it. Cheney had told them never to ask for volunteers for this job but to always use a fellow martial artist. The unpracticed board holder was apt to quail at the blow. If the board was moved away even slightly, it reduced the force of the blow and made it look as though it was the blow which failed.

Darius knelt and held a board. Troy raised a hand, then lowered it fiercely and split the board. The audience gasped in awe and shouted in pleasure.

170

"You see, I wasn't aiming *at* the board, but below it," Troy explained. Darius held another board and Troy swung his hand two feet below it to indicate where he was aiming. In rapid succession Darius picked up and held other boards and Troy split them. Left hand, right hand, left hand, right hand. Then he picked up a board, held it firmly, looked at the audience, and shook his head.

"He can't do it," he said of Darius. "He's not strong enough."

Darius split that board and continued, pow, pow, pow, as quickly as Troy picked them up, until there was only one board left. Troy moved it away before Darius could strike it.

"No, not this one," Troy said. "This is a magic board. I will show you its magic in a few minutes. Now we're going to give you a demonstration of the self-defense moves. In class we practice sparring between equals and unequals, and this, of course," he said, pointing to Darius' purple belt, "will be sparring between unequals. Because I'm tough, see, and I can dispatch him with ease."

He blustered up to Darius and Darius whirled and knocked him flat. He shook his head as though bewildered and came charging at Darius again. At every move Darius kicked, punched, blocked, dodged, and finally threw Troy over his back. The children roared and hollered for more. Darius bowed. Troy bowed. Darius bowed. Troy bowed. And suddenly Troy took hold of Darius and visited calamity on him.

"And that's the way it would really be between a brown belt and a purple belt," he said, dusting off his hands. Darius stood up and they bowed yet again while children, counselors, parents, clapped and clapped.

"Now for the finale," Troy said, "the magic board." He picked up the remaining, seemingly unbroken board and held it out. "I want one of you to break a board. Do I have a volunteer?" Some of the children shrank back a little and others clamored to be chosen. "How about you?" Troy said, choosing the smallest, scrawniest one, a boy about six who was in a tiny wheelchair. "You look tough and strong. Are you?"

The boy looked around to his friends and his counselor, who were saying, "Yeah, he's tough. He's strong." Then the boy said, "Yeah," and rolled his small chair forward.

"Remember what I told you? You don't aim *at* the board, but aim through it to two feet below it." The boy nodded. Troy reminded him how to hold his hand and reminded the others that they mustn't try it without training or without a magic board. "Ready?" He held the board steady. Just as the small hand was about to crash through it, Troy pulled the halves apart and held them up triumphantly. The other children roared with delight and the small boy reached for the broken board.

"For a souvenir," the boy said.

Troy handed it over to a chorus of "Me toos."

Darius was right there, passing out the other broken boards. Souvenirs. Troy had never thought of it.

As the boards were passed out, more applause burst and floated into the oaks. The clapping didn't resound as inside the karate or dance studio, but it resounded in Troy's ears. This time it was not like missiles but like garlands, like soft, sweet flowers landing all around him. These kids knew their own relentless fate, some of them standing, walking, but looking into their futures at the others in wheelchairs. And these kids were clapping for him. He'd given them something, some pleasure, some entertainment. Perhaps, he thought, he'd added to their vision that life *is*.

172

His body gave him one moment of warning that the emotions of the past thirty-two hours were about to erupt. He felt the surge and just had time to turn away. Children walked, rolled, or were rolled away one by one. Some of them, plus counselors and parents, started toward him to thank him and congratulate him. He heard Mom and Dad intercept them.

". . . involved in the bridge disaster last night," he heard them say.

Darius was with him, a hand on his shoulder, as he walked toward Golden River, which was part of the Intracoastal Waterway. He put an arm across his eyes to absorb his own waterway.

Cheney was there too, coming up on the other side and sliding an arm about him. "Troy, you have given more than I ever would have asked," Cheney said. "If it were possible to award the black belt without the test, you'd have it right now."

Troy barely heard Cheney's words.

"You were marvelous," Mother said, catching up with them.

"Yes, you were," said Dad, said Cheney, said Darius.

"I want to see Keven," Troy said. In his mind he knew that Keven was all right, but still stuck there in his guts was that time last night when he was certain Keven was dead. "I want to see Keven."

20

*S*o here, at last, were his mother and father at a karate tournament. Dad was immediately enchanted with the little ones and began snapping pictures. Nick and Keven had dragged their beleaguered bones and were also in the stands. Troy had told Cheney he'd take the black-belt test Monday night, and tomorrow, Sunday, he and Liesl were going to practice ballet. Life *is,* Troy thought.

Later in the morning, when Dad had climbed into the stands, Troy saw his father staring into space instead of watching the proceedings. Mother never took her eyes off the floor and Troy was jabbering, trying to explain the procedures. What was Dad seeing? Troy wondered. Sunsets and moonrise? Egrets drifting in to roost? Sea gulls riding thermals above the bridge? The bridge. Troy was going whole half-hours without thinking of it.

But at least Dad was here, and when Troy started out of the stands to do his kata, Dad followed, ready to take pictures. At last, Troy thought, there would be karate pictures. Troy in gi. Troy kicking. Troy punching. Troy spinning. On impulse, he turned and embraced his father. "I just remembered," he said. "I haven't hugged my dad today."

"Troy, be careful," Mother called.

He looked up at her. "This is just the kata, Mom. You don't have to close your eyes yet."

174

"You haven't told us what day it is," Keven called out.

No, he hadn't, and that was a fact. And he didn't remember telling anyone that yesterday was the beginning of unicorn-questing season. He looked up at Keven, so happy to see him there, with Nick, alive and well and still sassy.

"It's the Nottingham Goose Festival, you goose."